Echoes of the Fo

In the Shadows of a Cursed City, the Past Never Dies

Evelyn Harper

Copyright © 2024 by Evelyn Harper

All rights reserved. No part of this book may be used or reproduced in any form whatsoever without written permission except in the case of brief quotations in critical articles or reviews.

First Edition: November 2024

Table of Contents

Chapter 1 Shadows of Varunel 1

Chapter 2 Whispers in the Mist 19

Chapter 3 The Living Ruins 34

Chapter 4 Testing the Veil 52

Chapter 5 Echoes of the Past 68

Chapter 6 The Heart of Varunel 84

Chapter 7 The Shadow Within 100

Chapter 8 The Fragmented Path 114

Chapter 9 A Fateful Encounter 129

Chapter 10 Bonds in the Darkness 144

Chapter 11 The Waking Curse 160

Chapter 12 Truth in the Shadows 175

Chapter 13 Fractured Souls 189

Chapter 14 The Threshold of Despair 202

Chapter 15 The Last Whisper.. 215

Epilogue Beyond the Mist 226

Chapter 1
Shadows of Varunel

The air was heavier here, thick with an eerie quiet that seemed to press against the lungs, making every breath a conscious effort. The dirt road under Lira's boots was uneven, riddled with cracks and overgrown with weeds. Ahead, the outline of the city loomed, shrouded in a mist that pulsed faintly, almost like it had a life of its own. This was Varunel—a name whispered in fear and intrigue across the regions, its curse as infamous as the mysteries it guarded.

Kael adjusted the strap of his pack, the faint creak of leather breaking the silence as he studied the hazy outline of the Veiled Gates in the distance. The towering arches seemed carved out of shadow itself, rising from the earth like ancient sentinels. He glanced at Lira, who was a few paces ahead, her figure taut and deliberate as she surveyed their surroundings with sharp, practiced eyes.

"Well, this is cheery," Kael quipped, his voice breaking the oppressive stillness. "Nothing says 'welcome' like an unholy fog and a road that looks like it hasn't seen a carriage in decades."

Lira didn't turn. "The stories didn't lie about the mist. Seems thicker than it should be for this time of day."

Kael smirked, though it lacked his usual spark. "You're not about to tell me you're nervous, are you?"

"I don't get nervous," she replied evenly, though her gaze lingered on the shifting fog. "I get cautious. Big difference."

Kael fell into step beside her, his expression softening. "Cautious, sure. But this place—" He gestured broadly toward the encroaching haze, "—has all the charm of a graveyard. Even you have to admit it's unsettling."

Lira finally turned to look at him, her dark eyes steady. "It's a place. Just like any other. Only difference is the stories people tell to keep themselves entertained."

"Stories?" Kael echoed, raising an eyebrow. "Right, because ancient curses and disappearing townsfolk are just bedtime tales."

She shrugged, turning her attention back to the horizon. "Until I see proof otherwise, yes."

Kael chuckled under his breath, his tone tinged with disbelief. "You've got the emotional range of a brick wall, you know that? Doesn't anything about this place make your skin crawl? The gates, the fog, the fact that we haven't heard a single bird since we got here?"

"The quiet's unusual," she admitted, her voice still calm. "But I don't let my imagination run wild just because it's inconvenient. Stay focused, Kael."

"Focused," he repeated with a shake of his head. "Right. Focused on what, exactly? Wandering into the world's biggest death trap because of some vague rumors?"

Lira halted, turning to face him fully. Her gaze was sharp, cutting through the fog as much as it did through his words. "You know why we're here. You agreed to this."

"Agreed, sure," he replied, crossing his arms. "But don't pretend like we're on a casual stroll. We're walking into a cursed city with no clear idea of what we're up against."

Her expression hardened, but there was something beneath it—a flicker of something personal, raw. "I know what I'm up against."

Kael tilted his head, studying her with a mixture of curiosity and concern. "Do you, though? Because from where I'm standing, it feels like you're hoping for answers just as much as I am."

Lira's jaw tightened, and for a moment, she didn't respond. Instead, she turned back toward the path, her hand instinctively brushing the hilt of the blade strapped to her side. "This isn't about hope. It's about doing what needs to be done."

Kael frowned, but he let the silence stretch between them as they resumed walking. The road narrowed as the mist thickened, and the looming shape of the Veiled Gates grew clearer with each step. The towering stone arch was cracked and weathered, its surface etched with runes so faint they seemed more like scars than deliberate markings.

"I'll give it this much," Kael said quietly, breaking the silence again. "It's got an aesthetic. Gloomy, foreboding, maybe a little overdone. Perfect spot for some dramatic self-reflection."

Lira spared him a sidelong glance. "You always talk this much when you're nervous?"

Kael grinned, though it was fleeting. "Only when I know it annoys you."

They stopped a few paces from the gate, its dark surface looming above them like a reminder of every warning they'd ignored. Kael rested a hand on the weathered stone, feeling its chill seep through his gloves. "So… last chance to back out. We could always turn around and pretend we never got here."

"You could," Lira replied coolly, though the faintest hint of a smirk touched her lips. "But I'm not."

He let out a breath, his expression growing more serious. "Why is this so important to you, Lira? You never told me."

Her gaze remained on the gate, her shoulders stiff. "It's personal."

Kael waited, but when she didn't elaborate, he nodded slowly. "Fair enough. But whatever's waiting in there… we face it together, alright?"

For the first time, her expression softened, though her voice stayed firm. "We'll face it. But don't let the city get into your head. That's how it wins."

"Noted," he said, stepping back from the gate. "Shall we?"

Without waiting for a reply, Lira strode forward, her steps steady and deliberate. Kael followed close behind, his hand resting on the hilt of his blade as the mist swallowed them whole, leaving the Veiled Gates—and the world they knew—behind.

The Veiled Gates loomed overhead, massive and ancient, their cracked surface etched with fading runes that whispered of a forgotten time. As Lira and Kael stepped beneath the towering arch, the air shifted. The faint wind that had accompanied their journey disappeared, replaced by an oppressive stillness. The mist thickened, curling around their ankles and clinging to their clothes, like ghostly fingers intent on pulling them deeper.

Kael hesitated mid-step, glancing back at the gate. "It's quieter here," he said, his voice low. "Too quiet. You notice that?"

Lira didn't pause, her boots crunching softly on the gravel path ahead. "It's a city abandoned for decades, Kael. Quiet comes with the territory."

"No, it's not just quiet," he said, quickening his pace to match hers. "It's… wrong. Like the air's holding its breath."

She stopped, turning to face him. "The air doesn't breathe. It's your imagination."

Kael gestured toward the swirling mist that seemed to move against the windless atmosphere. "My imagination's not making that fog act like it's alive. Look at it—it's moving toward us."

Lira crossed her arms, tilting her head slightly as she examined the fog. "Mist is drawn to pressure changes. Could be a shift in temperature. Nothing supernatural about that."

Kael threw up his hands. "Of course. Mist physics. Should've known you'd have an answer for everything."

"It's called logic," Lira replied, turning and continuing down the path. "Try it sometime."

Kael sighed, following her reluctantly. "Logic's overrated when the place looks like it's straight out of a ghost story."

The mist thickened as they moved farther into the city, swallowing the light and dampening the sound of their footsteps. Kael's gaze darted from one shadowy outline to another. The faint silhouettes of buildings emerged and disappeared in the fog, their jagged edges softened but no less foreboding. What little light filtered through the mist seemed to bend, pooling in unnatural ways that made it hard to discern distances.

"So," Kael began, his tone forced and light, "remind me why we're walking straight into the fog of doom instead of, say, waiting for backup? Or, hear me out—running in the opposite direction."

"Because waiting doesn't get answers," Lira replied without looking back. "And running is for people who don't know how to face a challenge."

"Oh, I can face a challenge just fine," he said, quickening his pace to walk beside her. "But wandering into a cursed city where no one's ever come back? That's not a challenge, Lira. That's a death wish."

Lira's lips twitched in what might have been amusement. "You came anyway."

"Only because I'm worried you'll get yourself killed without me," he shot back, though there was no heat in his voice. "Admit it—you need me here to keep you grounded."

"Grounded?" Lira raised an eyebrow. "Coming from the guy who thinks fog has a vendetta?"

Kael stopped, pointing at the twisted remains of what looked like a lamppost emerging from the mist. Its once-sturdy base was rusted and bent, the lantern shattered and dangling by a single chain. "That's not just fog, Lira. Look around. Everything here feels... off. Like time stopped but forgot to tell the city."

She glanced at the lamppost, her expression impassive. "It's decay. That happens when places are abandoned."

"And the silence?" he pressed. "The way sound doesn't carry here? Or how the mist feels like it's watching us?"

"It's your nerves," she said simply, resuming her pace. "This place is designed to make people uneasy. That's how the stories start—people let their imagination do the work."

Kael ran a hand through his hair, muttering under his breath. "Right. Imagination. Sure."

They passed a crumbling fountain, its centerpiece obscured by moss and streaks of grime. Water no longer flowed, but a faint sound of dripping echoed faintly, as if the city itself couldn't let go of its memories. Kael slowed, staring at the fountain.

"Do you hear that?" he asked, his voice barely above a whisper.

Lira stopped, listening for a moment before shaking her head. "No."

Kael stepped closer, pointing toward the basin. "There's a sound. Dripping. But there's no water."

"Probably condensation," she said. "Or the wind."

"There's no wind," Kael said sharply, turning to face her. "And you know it."

Her eyes narrowed slightly. "Don't start."

"I'm not starting anything," he said, his tone rising. "But you can't keep brushing this off. You feel it too, don't you? That… wrongness."

Lira's jaw tightened. "I feel a lot of things. Fear isn't one of them."

"That's not what I said," Kael replied, his voice softening. "You can call it fear, nerves, whatever you want. But this place… it's not just a bunch of crumbling buildings."

"Then what is it?" she challenged, stepping closer. "A ghost? A curse? Come on, Kael. You're better than this."

Kael hesitated, then looked away. "I don't know what it is. But it's something."

Lira sighed, her shoulders relaxing slightly. "Something doesn't hold weight. Keep your focus. Let's move."

Kael lingered by the fountain for a moment before falling back into step beside her. "You keep saying 'focus.' Fine. But if we're ignoring what we feel, how are we supposed to stay sharp?"

She glanced at him, her expression unreadable. "By remembering why we're here. Keep your mind on the objective, not the fog."

Kael nodded, though his unease didn't fade. As they moved deeper into the city, the mist thickened further, and the silence wrapped around them like a shroud. Whatever lay ahead, neither of them could deny that Varunel wasn't just a city—it was waiting.

The mist seemed to thicken with every step, clinging to their skin and clothes like a damp shroud. Lira's boots scuffed against the uneven stones of the pathway as she scanned the swirling fog ahead. Kael trailed slightly behind, his gaze darting nervously to the shifting shadows that seemed to lurk just beyond their reach.

"You're awfully quiet," Lira said without looking back. "Finally running out of things to say?"

"Just trying not to breathe too deeply," Kael muttered. "Feels like this fog might crawl inside and start unpacking."

Lira smirked faintly. "If the fog kills you, it'll be for whining too much."

"Ha. Ha." Kael squinted into the haze ahead. "Seriously, though. You don't feel it? Like we're being—"

"Watched?" Lira interrupted, her tone matter-of-fact. "Yes. But that's just nerves."

Before Kael could respond, the fog shifted. It was subtle at first—a deepening of the shadows, a faint ripple in the air—but then it parted abruptly, revealing a figure standing directly in their path. Lira's hand instinctively dropped to the hilt of her blade, her body tensing. Kael froze, his breath catching.

The figure was an old woman, draped in tattered layers of cloth that seemed more like an extension of the fog itself. Her face was pale and lined, her eyes sharp and unsettlingly bright against the surrounding gloom. She moved without a sound, as if the ground itself yielded to her presence.

"Welcome to Varunel," the woman said, her voice a rasping whisper that carried with unnatural clarity. "You have come for answers, have you not?"

Lira held her ground, her grip steady on her blade. "Who are you?"

The woman tilted her head, her expression unreadable. "I am Elder Thorne, a keeper of sorts. And you are trespassers, though the city seems to have allowed you entry."

"Allowed us?" Kael echoed, his voice cracking slightly. "Pretty sure we just walked in."

"Nothing in Varunel is ever so simple," Thorne said with a faint smile that didn't reach her eyes. She took a step closer, her gaze flicking between them. "You should not have come."

"Yet here we are," Lira said sharply, her voice cutting through the fog. "What do you know about this place?"

Thorne regarded her for a moment, then reached into the folds of her tattered clothing. Her hand emerged holding a small, tarnished object—a talisman etched with symbols that seemed to shift in the dim light. In her other hand, she produced a piece of parchment, its edges frayed and curling.

"This," Thorne said, holding out the objects, "may help you survive. If you are wise."

Lira hesitated, then stepped forward to take the items. Her fingers brushed against the talisman's cool surface, and a strange, tingling sensation shot up her arm. She glanced at the parchment, noting the hand-drawn lines and symbols that formed an intricate map.

"What's this?" she asked, her tone cautious.

"A map," Thorne replied. "And a guide. It will show you the paths you must take, but it will not protect you. The talisman will."

Kael leaned closer, peering at the objects with open suspicion. "Protect us from what?"

Thorne's gaze snapped to him, her expression suddenly sharp. "From the city. Varunel listens. It whispers. And when it knows your fears, it will twist them against you."

Kael swallowed hard, his earlier bravado all but gone. "Great. So, a haunted city and an evil fog. Anything else we should know?"

Thorne's lips curved into a grim smile. "Yes. The city does not forget. It remembers every soul that has walked its streets, every voice that has cried out within its walls. And it hungers for more."

"Why let us in at all, then?" Lira asked, her voice steady despite the unease creeping into her chest. "If it's so dangerous, why not warn us off?"

Thorne studied her for a long moment, her expression softening into something almost mournful. "Because some curses can only be broken by those who do not belong. And some sacrifices… are necessary."

Kael's jaw tightened. "That's reassuring."

Lira tucked the talisman and map into her pack, her movements deliberate. "We're not here to be sacrifices. We're here for answers."

Thorne's eyes gleamed with something unreadable—pity, perhaps, or resignation. "Then tread carefully, wanderers. The city will offer you answers, yes. But it will demand a price. Be certain you are willing to pay it."

"We'll manage," Lira said curtly, stepping past the old woman.

Kael hesitated, his gaze lingering on Thorne. "You're not coming with us?"

"I cannot," Thorne said simply, fading back into the mist. "This is not my path to walk."

Before Kael could respond, the fog closed around her, swallowing her entirely. He blinked, staring at the empty space where she'd stood.

"Great," he muttered, turning to follow Lira. "So now we've got a haunted city *and* a cryptic old lady. This just keeps getting better."

"Focus, Kael," Lira said without looking back, her tone sharper than usual. "We have what we need. Let's move."

Kael fell silent, his unease palpable as they continued into the mist. The talisman felt heavy in Lira's pack, its presence a constant reminder of Thorne's warning. Though her expression remained composed, a small voice in the back of her mind whispered that they were being watched—and that the price Thorne spoke of might be higher than they were prepared to pay.

The mist curled around them as they walked, thickening with every step. The talisman seemed to radiate a faint, icy chill through Lira's pack, a subtle but constant reminder of the warnings Elder Thorne had given. Kael cast a glance over his shoulder, the Veiled Gates now fully swallowed by the fog. They were alone—or at least, it felt that way.

"This city," Kael said, breaking the silence, "it's not just a place, is it?"

Lira's pace didn't falter. "What else would it be?"

Kael quickened his steps to keep up, his boots crunching against the loose gravel. "You heard what Thorne said. It listens. It remembers. That doesn't sound like a regular city to me."

"Sounds like a lot of superstition," Lira replied flatly. "She's been out here too long, probably feeding on her own fear."

"Right. And the moving mist? The creepy silence? Just explainable phenomena, huh?"

"Exactly," she said without hesitation. "The mist is dense, the air dampens sound, and fear does the rest. It's basic psychology."

Kael let out a dry laugh, gesturing to the swirling fog around them. "Oh, sure. 'Basic psychology.' I'm sure the ominous fog that moves like it has a mind of its own is just my imagination. What about the talisman? You think that's just a fancy trinket?"

Lira didn't answer immediately, her eyes scanning their path. The broken remnants of buildings loomed faintly in the mist, their jagged edges softened by decay. "It's a precaution," she said finally. "Thorne believes it has power, and if it keeps her alive out here, I'm not going to throw it away."

Kael stopped, planting his hands on his hips. "So you do believe there's something to it."

She turned, her expression calm but firm. "I believe in being prepared."

"And if she's right? About the city? About the curse?" he pressed, his voice rising. "What if this place really does twist people's fears into something... worse?"

Lira's gaze didn't waver. "Then we stay sharp and stick to the plan. Letting fear control us is what gets people killed."

Kael ran a hand through his hair, frustration creeping into his voice. "You can't just dismiss everything as 'fear.' There's something real here, Lira. I can feel it. And I know you feel it too."

"What I feel," she said, her tone sharpening, "is the weight of a mission. A mission that doesn't care about how I feel."

Kael stepped closer, lowering his voice. "You're not a machine, Lira. Ignoring what's in front of you doesn't make it less real. It makes you blind."

She crossed her arms, her posture stiffening. "And jumping at every shadow makes you reckless. Which one do you think gets us out of here alive?"

His jaw tightened, and for a moment, the air between them crackled with unspoken tension. Finally, Kael exhaled, glancing away. "Alright. Fine. You're the boss. We do it your way."

Lira studied him for a moment, her expression softening slightly. "It's not about being the boss. It's about staying focused. Whatever's out here, real or not, we can't let it distract us."

Kael's lips twitched into a faint, humorless smile. "You're good at that. Staying focused."

"It's kept me alive this long," she replied. "And it'll keep us alive too, if you trust me."

He nodded reluctantly. "I trust you. I just… I can't shake the feeling that this place isn't just dangerous. It's personal."

Lira's brow furrowed at his words, but she didn't respond. Instead, she turned and began walking again, her steps steady and deliberate. Kael hesitated, glancing back at the fog that seemed to close in behind them, then followed.

The city seemed to shift subtly as they moved deeper. Shadows lengthened and twisted, forming vague, fleeting shapes that disappeared as quickly as they appeared. The silence grew heavier, pressing against their ears until even their own footsteps seemed muted.

Kael broke the quiet again. "You ever think about why this place exists? Why it's the way it is?"

Lira kept her eyes forward. "No."

"Really?" he pressed. "Not even a little curiosity?"

"Curiosity doesn't get the job done," she said. "Answers come after we finish the mission."

Kael frowned. "And if the mission *is* the answer?"

Lira paused, turning to face him. "Then we'll find out. But not by standing around asking questions we can't answer."

Her words were firm, but there was a flicker of something in her eyes—something she quickly masked. Kael opened his mouth to respond but thought better of it. Instead, he fell into step beside her, the weight of Thorne's warnings hanging heavily between them.

As they continued, the fog seemed to part slightly, revealing the faint outlines of a crumbling street stretching ahead. Lira slowed, her gaze narrowing. "We keep moving. No detours, no distractions."

"Got it," Kael said, though his tone was subdued. "No distractions."

Despite his agreement, his eyes lingered on the shifting shadows, his unease growing with every step. The city whispered to him, faint and insistent, a voice just beyond comprehension. He shook his head, trying to shake off the feeling, and focused on Lira's steady presence ahead.

Whatever secrets Varunel held, they would face them together. Whether they were ready for what awaited was another question entirely.

Chapter 2
Whispers in the Mist

The mist thickened as Lira and Kael pressed deeper into the abandoned streets of Varunel, its heavy tendrils curling around them like smoke. The city felt alive, its oppressive silence broken only by the faint sound of their footsteps against cracked stone. But then the whispers began again—soft, insidious murmurs that seemed to weave through the fog.

Kael stopped abruptly, his hand instinctively going to the hilt of his blade. "Did you hear that?" he asked, his voice low.

Lira glanced over her shoulder, her expression unreadable. "Hear what?"

"The whispers," Kael said, his eyes narrowing as he scanned the mist. "They're getting louder."

"It's the wind," Lira replied, her tone clipped as she kept walking. "Nothing to worry about."

Kael didn't move immediately, his brow furrowing. "That's not wind, Lira. That's… something else. I swear I heard—" He stopped, his voice trailing off as the whispers came again. This time, they were clearer, weaving fragmented syllables into what sounded like… names.

"Kael…" The word slithered through the fog, faint but unmistakable.

He stiffened, his blood running cold. "It said my name."

Lira stopped and turned, annoyance flashing in her eyes. "It didn't."

"It did," Kael insisted, stepping toward her. "I know what I heard."

"It's just echoes," Lira said, her voice firm. "Sounds bouncing off the ruins. This place is full of cracks and crevices—it's acoustics, not magic."

Kael shook his head, his grip tightening on his weapon. "No. This is something else. You didn't hear it?"

"I hear everything you hear," she said, crossing her arms. "I just don't let it get to me."

"It's not about letting it get to me," Kael argued, his voice rising slightly. "It said my name, Lira. That's not something echoes do."

"Exactly," she shot back. "It's not real. This city is trying to mess with us. Don't let it."

Before Kael could respond, the whispers shifted again, growing louder. The indistinct murmurs coalesced into words, their tones sharper, more urgent.

"Turn… back…"

Kael froze, the blood draining from his face. He turned slowly toward the sound, his heart pounding. "Did you hear that?" he asked again, his voice barely above a whisper.

Lira sighed, her grip tightening on her blade. "Yes. And I'm still not stopping."

"It's a warning," Kael said, his tone desperate. "Lira, what if this place is alive? What if it's trying to tell us something?"

"It's not alive," she said firmly. "It's a city. Cities don't think, and they don't talk."

"Then what is it?" Kael asked, stepping closer to her. "Because those voices aren't just noise. They're… deliberate. They know our names, Lira."

"That's exactly why you need to ignore them," she snapped. "This place feeds on fear. The more you listen, the more power you give it."

Kael exhaled sharply, his frustration mounting. "You're so sure of that, aren't you? That it's all in my head. What if you're wrong? What if this place really is alive, and it's warning us for a reason?"

Lira's gaze hardened. "Then we'll deal with it when it tries to stop us. Until then, keep walking."

Kael hesitated, glancing back into the mist. The whispers had quieted again, retreating into the oppressive silence. But the weight of their words lingered, coiled tightly around his chest like a vice. "You're acting like this is normal," he muttered as he caught up to her.

"It is," Lira said without looking back. "For a cursed city."

Kael let out a bitter laugh, shaking his head. "You don't even believe in curses."

"And I don't need to," she replied sharply. "I believe in staying alive. That's all that matters."

The conversation ended as abruptly as it had begun, both of them falling into uneasy silence. The path ahead was barely visible through the fog, the ruins looming like broken teeth against the gray sky. Kael kept his blade close, his eyes darting to every shifting shadow, every flicker of movement in the corners of his vision.

But the whispers didn't return—not yet. Instead, the city seemed to hold its breath, waiting. Kael couldn't shake the feeling that they weren't just walking through Varunel—they were walking into something.

And whatever it was, it knew their names.

The whispers grew louder, their words still indistinct but pressing, as though the city itself were speaking directly into their minds. The mist swirled thicker, curling tightly around Lira and Kael, almost as if it were trying to suffocate them. Kael tightened his grip on his blade, his breath quickening as his eyes darted toward the shifting shadows.

"Lira," he said, his voice strained. "We can't keep walking like this. We need to do something."

Lira shot him a sharp glance, irritation flickering in her eyes. "What do you suggest? Have a heart-to-heart with the fog?"

Kael ignored her sarcasm, his gaze dropping to the talisman hanging around her neck. The metal caught the faint light of the mist, its intricate carvings glowing faintly as though alive. "The talisman," he said, gesturing toward it. "Let's test it."

She frowned, stepping back slightly. "Test it? On what?"

"The whispers," Kael said, his voice firm. "You heard what Elder Thorne said. It's supposed to protect us, right? Let's see if it actually does."

Lira shook her head, her hand moving instinctively to the talisman. "This thing is just an old relic. It doesn't do anything."

"You don't know that," Kael argued. "We've barely used it. What if it's the only thing keeping us safe?"

Lira let out a sharp breath, her grip tightening around the talisman. "We don't even know how it works, Kael. For all we know, it's just a piece of metal with fancy carvings."

"And what if it's not?" Kael countered, stepping closer. "What if it's the only reason we've made it this far? Come on, Lira. What's the harm in trying?"

She hesitated, her eyes narrowing as she studied his face. The determination in his expression gave her pause, but she still looked unconvinced. "Fine," she said grudgingly, pulling the talisman from around her neck. "But when this does nothing, I don't want to hear any more about it."

Kael took the talisman carefully, his fingers brushing the cool surface. The carvings seemed to hum faintly against his skin, a subtle vibration that made him shiver. He held it up, turning it toward the mist.

"Alright," he said quietly. "Let's see what happens."

The whispers swirled louder, almost mocking, as Kael raised the talisman higher. Then, abruptly, they stopped. The silence was so sudden, so absolute, that it felt like the air had been sucked out of the space around them. The mist pulled back slightly, revealing more of the ruined street ahead. Kael and Lira exchanged a look, both frozen in place.

"Did you—" Kael began, but Lira cut him off.

"It's a coincidence," she said quickly, her voice sharp. "Nothing more."

Kael frowned, lowering the talisman slightly. The whispers began to creep back in, faint at first but growing louder with every second. He raised the talisman again, and once more, the sound ceased, the mist retreating just enough to make the space feel breathable.

"It's not a coincidence, Lira," Kael said firmly. "This thing works. It's protecting us."

Lira's jaw tightened, her eyes flicking to the talisman. "Or the city's just toying with us. You can't trust anything here, Kael. Not even that."

"You don't believe that," he said, stepping closer. "I saw your face. You felt it, didn't you?"

"What I felt doesn't matter," she said sharply. "What matters is that we don't let this place mess with our heads."

Kael let out a frustrated breath, lowering the talisman again. The whispers surged back almost instantly, louder and angrier than before. He flinched at the sound, then raised the talisman once more, silencing them again.

"You can't ignore this," he said, his tone softer now. "This isn't just some random trinket, Lira. It's real. And it's keeping us alive."

She crossed her arms, her expression unreadable. "Even if it is, we can't rely on it. What happens when it stops working? What happens when it's not enough?"

Kael hesitated, his grip on the talisman tightening. "Then we figure it out. But right now, this is the only thing keeping us from going insane. You can't just brush that off."

Lira looked away, her jaw tightening. For a moment, she said nothing, her thoughts churning behind her guarded expression. Then she sighed, holding out her hand. "Fine. Give it back."

Kael hesitated, then handed the talisman to her. The whispers immediately surged louder, and she flinched, the sound slicing through the air like nails on a chalkboard. As soon as she slipped the talisman back around her neck, the noise stopped, and the mist pulled back slightly again.

"Happy now?" she asked, her tone biting but quieter.

Kael smiled faintly, his tension easing. "Not happy. But I think we just figured out what's keeping us sane."

She shot him a glare, then turned back toward the path ahead. "Don't get used to it. This thing's not magic. It's just buying us time."

"Time's enough," Kael said, following her. "For now."

They moved forward, the mist parting slightly with each step. But the whispers lingered at the edge of the silence, waiting for the moment they would falter again.

The whispers returned with a vengeance, threading through the thick mist like invisible claws. The voices were louder now, more insistent, and no longer content to hover on the edges of their awareness. They pressed inward, surrounding Lira and Kael with an oppressive, suffocating weight.

Lira clenched her jaw, her hand gripping the hilt of her blade tightly. Her pace quickened, as if she could outrun the sound.

"Lira," Kael called from behind her, his voice barely audible over the rising cacophony. "Wait."

She ignored him, her gaze fixed ahead, though the shadows and fog offered no clear path forward. The whispers clawed at her mind, her name slipping through their disjointed phrases like venom. Her hands trembled despite her best efforts to steady them.

"Lira!" Kael's voice was louder now, firm but tinged with concern. He jogged to catch up, stepping in front of her and forcing her to stop. "Hey, slow down. What's going on?"

"Nothing," she snapped, her tone sharper than intended. "We don't have time to stop."

Kael frowned, studying her. Her face was pale, her breathing uneven, and her eyes darted restlessly toward every shifting shadow. "You're shaking," he said softly. "Talk to me."

"I'm fine," she bit out, sidestepping him and continuing forward. "Keep moving."

"You're not fine," he said, stepping in front of her again. His voice dropped, steady but firm. "Lira, stop. Just for a second."

She glared at him, frustration flickering in her eyes. "What do you want me to say, Kael? That this place is getting to me? That I can't stand the constant noise? Fine. You're right. Now let me do my job."

Kael hesitated, taken aback by her outburst. "I'm not trying to get in your way. I just think we need to—"

"To what?" she interrupted, her voice rising. "To stop and sit down in the middle of this cursed city? To listen to the whispers and let them tear us apart?"

"That's not what I'm saying," he replied calmly, his hands raised slightly in a placating gesture. "But you can't keep pushing yourself like this. It's not just about surviving—it's about staying sane."

She let out a harsh laugh, the sound brittle and bitter. "Sanity went out the window the moment we stepped into this place. The only thing keeping us alive is not letting it win."

Kael sighed, his gaze softening. "And how long do you think you can keep that up? Pretending nothing bothers you?"

"I don't have a choice," she said through gritted teeth. "If I fall apart, we both die. So excuse me if I don't have time to talk about my feelings."

Kael studied her for a moment, his expression unreadable. Then he stepped aside, giving her a clear path forward. "Alright," he said quietly. "If you really think running yourself into the ground is the only way to get through this, go ahead."

She hesitated, the sudden lack of resistance catching her off guard. Her fingers twitched at her sides, brushing the hilt of her blade. "Kael, don't start—"

"I'm not starting anything," he interrupted, his tone even but firm. "I'm just saying you're not as invincible as you think you are. And that's okay. But if you keep acting like you are, it's going to get us both killed."

Her gaze flicked to his, her jaw tightening. For a moment, her walls cracked, and he saw the fear and exhaustion she'd been trying so hard to bury. Then she straightened, her expression hardening once more. "We don't have time for this," she said, her voice quieter but no less resolute. "Let's move."

Kael sighed, running a hand through his hair. "Fine. But this isn't over."

"Good," she shot back, stepping past him. "Because neither are we."

The whispers seemed to surge again, as if mocking her defiance. Lira's hand drifted to the talisman at her neck, her fingers brushing the cold metal. It offered little comfort, but it was enough to keep her moving. Kael followed silently, his concern for her growing with each step.

The mist thickened once more, swallowing the street ahead. And though they walked side by side, the distance between them felt wider than ever.

The mist was so dense now that it was impossible to see more than a few steps ahead. Each footfall echoed eerily, the sound swallowed almost immediately by the oppressive silence of

Varunel. Lira led the way, her hand hovering near her blade, her eyes darting to every flicker of movement in the fog. Kael followed closely, his grip tightening around the talisman in his pocket, its faint vibration a constant reminder of its significance.

"Lira," Kael said, his voice cutting through the heavy air. "We can't even see where we're going. This is reckless."

"We don't have time to waste," she replied sharply, her tone brooking no argument. "The longer we wait, the worse this place gets."

Kael stopped walking, frustration bubbling to the surface. "And charging blindly into the mist is better? You don't even know what's ahead."

She turned to face him, her expression hard. "I know what's behind us. More whispers, more shadows, more traps. If you want to stand here and wait for the city to swallow you whole, be my guest. But I'm moving forward."

Kael let out a breath, shaking his head. "Do you ever stop to think, just for a second, that this isn't about speed? That maybe we need to be careful?"

"We don't have the luxury of being careful," she shot back. "Every minute we waste standing still, this place gets stronger."

"It's not about standing still," he said, stepping closer. "It's about staying alive. You think plowing ahead without a plan is going to help us?"

Before she could respond, the shadows around them shifted. The mist thinned just enough to reveal a collapsed building to their left, its jagged edges jutting into the fog like broken bones. The faint light from their surroundings seemed to warp and bend, casting unnatural, flickering shapes along the walls.

Kael's gaze snapped to the movement, his hand going to his blade. "Did you see that?"

"I saw it," Lira said, her voice low and steady. She stepped toward the building, her body tense. "Stay close."

Kael grabbed her arm, stopping her. "Wait. We don't know what's in there."

"That's why I'm going to check," she said, pulling free. "The only way out of this city is through it."

"And what if this is another one of its traps?" Kael demanded, his voice rising. "What if it's waiting for us to walk right in?"

"Then we spring the trap," she replied coldly. "Better that than sitting here waiting for it to find us."

Kael stared at her, his frustration mounting. "You can't keep thinking like that, Lira. Not every fight is worth picking."

"And not every fight can be avoided," she said, stepping closer to the building. Her voice softened slightly, though her resolve didn't waver. "We don't have a choice, Kael. If we hesitate, we die."

Before Kael could argue further, the talisman pulsed faintly in his hand, the vibration growing stronger as they neared the collapsed building. He glanced down at it, his breath catching. "It's reacting."

Lira stopped, her gaze flicking to the talisman. "What do you mean?"

Kael held it up, the carvings glowing faintly in the dim light. "It's stronger here. Like it's... warning us."

Lira's jaw tightened, her eyes scanning the shadows. "Or guiding us."

"Or leading us straight into danger," Kael countered. "We don't know what this thing wants."

She turned to him, her expression unreadable. "We don't know what *anything* here wants. But this is the only lead we have."

Kael hesitated, his fingers tightening around the talisman. The shadows along the building's walls flickered again, their movements almost human. He exhaled slowly. "Fine. But we stick together. No splitting up."

"Agreed," Lira said, her tone clipped. She drew her blade, her posture tense as she stepped toward the building. "Stay behind me."

Kael followed, his hand on his weapon, the talisman glowing steadily in his other hand. The closer they got, the more the air seemed to hum with energy. The shadows moved faster now, darting along the walls in chaotic patterns. The whispers returned, louder this time, their words barely discernible.

"Turn… away…"

Lira stopped at the entrance of the building, her shoulders stiffening. She glanced at Kael, her expression grim. "Ready?"

"No," he said honestly, his voice tight. "But let's do it anyway."

She smirked faintly, though it didn't reach her eyes. "That's the spirit."

Together, they stepped into the darkness, the talisman's glow the only light guiding their way. The shadows closed in around them, the whispers rising to a deafening crescendo. And as they disappeared into the heart of the building, the city seemed to hold its breath, waiting for its next move.

Chapter 3
The Living Ruins

The city center loomed ahead, barely visible through the dense mist that seemed to press inward with every step. The once-spacious streets narrowed as if the city itself were shifting, forcing Lira and Kael toward a focal point. The oppressive fog clung to their skin, damp and cold, and the faint smell of mildew and decay hung in the air. Kael's breathing grew heavier, his posture tense as he followed closely behind Lira.

"Are we getting closer, or is this place just messing with us?" Kael asked, his voice strained as he glanced around, searching for landmarks in the swirling haze.

"We're on track," Lira said without turning. Her voice was steady, but there was an edge to it, as if she were trying to convince herself as much as him.

"On track to what, exactly?" Kael stopped, gesturing at the mist that seemed to pulse like a living thing. "This city doesn't feel like it's letting us anywhere. It feels like it's—"

"Don't say it," Lira cut him off, her tone sharp.

"—watching us," he finished, ignoring her warning. His eyes darted to the fog, narrowing at the way it curled and shifted in response to their movements. "You see it too, don't you? It's not just fog. It moves… like it's alive."

Lira sighed, turning to face him. "We've been over this. It's mist. The way it moves is a trick of the wind."

"There's no wind," Kael shot back, his frustration evident. "And don't tell me it's my imagination. You're seeing the same thing I am."

She hesitated for a fraction of a second, her gaze flicking toward the mist. It curled inward slightly, almost as if it were reacting to their voices. Lira clenched her jaw and shook her head.

"It doesn't matter what it looks like," she said firmly. "What matters is that we keep moving. Standing here debating isn't going to help."

Kael laughed bitterly, throwing up his hands. "Of course not. Why would stopping to figure out if the city's trying to eat us be helpful?"

Lira stepped closer, her voice low but cutting. "Focus, Kael. That's what's going to keep us alive. Not paranoia."

"Paranoia?" Kael's voice rose, his anxiety spilling over. "I'm not paranoid. I'm cautious. There's a difference."

"And I'm telling you, the city is playing tricks on us. If you start questioning every shadow, every movement, we'll never make it through."

Kael fell silent for a moment, studying her face. Her expression was as calm and composed as ever, but there was something in her eyes—a flicker of doubt, quickly suppressed. He pointed at her, his tone softer but insistent.

"You don't believe that, do you? Not entirely. I can see it. This place is getting to you too."

Lira's shoulders stiffened, but she didn't deny it. Instead, she turned away and began walking again, her pace brisk. "We're wasting time."

Kael groaned but followed, muttering under his breath. "Fine. Let's waste time walking into whatever trap this city's setting up for us instead."

As they moved closer to what appeared to be the center of the city, the fog thickened, wrapping around them like a cocoon. The faint outline of a plaza came into view, the crumbling remnants of a fountain standing at its center. The mist coiled around the fountain, its movements unnervingly deliberate.

"This is it?" Kael asked, glancing at the fountain. "The big city center?"

Lira nodded, scanning the area. "This is where the map leads."

Kael looked at her sharply. "And now what? You think we'll find answers just sitting here waiting for the mist to talk?"

"Maybe," Lira said simply, moving toward the fountain. "Or maybe this is where we start looking for clues."

Kael stayed back, his hand resting on the hilt of his blade. "This place doesn't feel like it wants to give us anything. Feels more like it's trying to bury us."

Lira knelt by the fountain, her fingers brushing against the worn stone. For a moment, her expression softened, a flicker of something unreadable passing over her face. She hesitated, then pulled back abruptly.

Kael frowned. "What was that?"

"Nothing," she said quickly, standing and brushing off her hands.

"That wasn't nothing," Kael pressed, stepping closer. "You froze. What did you see?"

Lira didn't meet his gaze. "I didn't see anything. It's just… familiar."

"Familiar?" Kael's eyebrows shot up. "Lira, if there's something you're not telling me—"

"There's nothing to tell," she snapped, cutting him off. "We're here for answers. That's all that matters."

Kael stared at her, his frustration mounting. "You're acting like this isn't personal for you. But it is, isn't it?"

Lira clenched her fists, her voice dropping to a whisper. "I don't have time for personal."

Kael opened his mouth to argue, but the mist shifted again, pulling their attention back to the plaza. A faint noise echoed through the fog—soft, almost imperceptible, like a breath exhaled in the silence.

"What now?" Kael muttered, drawing his blade.

Lira stepped forward, her own hand resting on the hilt of her weapon. "We keep moving. And we don't let it see that we're afraid."

Kael gave her a wry smile. "Speak for yourself."

"Just follow me," Lira said, her voice steady but quieter than usual.

As they moved deeper into the plaza, the mist seemed to tighten around them, as if testing their resolve. Lira kept her eyes ahead, her mind racing with memories she couldn't quite place. Whatever connection she had to this place, she wasn't ready to confront it—not yet. For now, all that mattered was staying ahead of the city's unseen dangers.

The fog thickened around them, its density swallowing the weak light that filtered through the ruins. Each step forward was slower than the last, the oppressive silence broken only by their muted footsteps. The air was damp and cold, and Kael couldn't shake the feeling that it wasn't just the mist pressing in—it was something else. Something alive.

Lira moved ahead, her steps deliberate, her focus unwavering. She didn't speak, but her hand hovered near her blade, her posture tense. Kael followed, his eyes scanning the haze. He froze suddenly, grabbing her arm.

"Lira, wait."

She stopped, turning to face him with a sharp look. "What?"

He didn't answer immediately. Instead, he pointed into the fog, where a faint shape was beginning to emerge. It was barely more than an outline, but it was unmistakably human—a figure standing still, just out of reach.

"You see that?" Kael's voice was barely above a whisper.

Lira squinted, her grip tightening on her blade. "It's just the mist."

Kael shook his head. "No, it's not. Look at it—it's moving."

The figure shifted slightly, its head tilting as though it were watching them. Kael stepped back, his hand moving to his weapon. Lira didn't move, her eyes narrowing as the figure dissolved into the fog as quickly as it had appeared.

"It's a trick," she said firmly, though her voice carried an edge. "The mist plays with the light."

Kael let out a shaky laugh. "Yeah, because light always bends into the shape of creepy shadow people."

She turned to him, her gaze sharp. "Focus. This is what the city wants—distraction."

Before he could respond, another figure appeared, this time to their right. Then another, to the left. The shapes were faint, more shadow than substance, but there was something unnervingly deliberate about the way they lingered just out of reach. Kael's breath quickened.

"Lira," he said, his voice tight, "they're everywhere."

"They're not real," she snapped, though her eyes flicked nervously between the figures. "Just illusions."

Kael took a step closer to her, his voice rising. "Illusions don't move like that. They're watching us. You can't tell me you don't see it."

She hesitated, her jaw tightening. The shadows were growing more defined, their movements slow but purposeful. Lira gripped the talisman hanging from her neck, the metal cold against her skin. The weight of it seemed to ground her, though the unease in her chest didn't fade.

Kael noticed her clutching the talisman and frowned. "What are you doing?"

"Testing a theory," she muttered.

"What theory?"

She didn't answer. Instead, she held the talisman aloft, its etched surface glinting faintly in the dim light. The air around them seemed to shift, the fog pulling back slightly. The figures hesitated, their movements stuttering before they dissolved into the mist.

Kael stared, his expression a mixture of relief and disbelief. "Did that just—"

"It's a coincidence," Lira said quickly, tucking the talisman back into her pack. "The mist shifted, that's all."

Kael let out a disbelieving laugh. "You're kidding, right? That thing just scared them off."

"They weren't real," she said sharply. "You can't scare off something that doesn't exist."

"They were real enough to watch us," Kael shot back, gesturing to the empty space where the figures had been. "And whatever they were, your little trinket just sent them packing."

Lira ignored him, her focus shifting back to the path ahead. "We keep moving."

Kael grabbed her arm, forcing her to stop. "Lira, you can't just brush this off. You saw what happened. The talisman works."

"Maybe it does," she admitted reluctantly. "But that doesn't mean the shadows were anything more than tricks of the light."

Kael stared at her, his frustration evident. "Why do you always do this? Why can't you just admit something's wrong here?"

"Because admitting it doesn't help," she snapped, pulling her arm free. "What helps is staying calm and finishing the mission."

He fell silent, his jaw tightening as he watched her walk away. The fog swirled around them, shifting as though it were alive, and he couldn't shake the feeling that the shadows were still there, just waiting for the right moment to reappear.

As he caught up to her, he glanced at the talisman, now hidden beneath her coat. "You're still holding onto it."

She didn't look at him. "It's insurance."

"For something you don't believe in?"

"For something I'm not taking chances with," she replied, her voice quieter now.

Kael nodded slowly, his grip tightening on his blade. "Fair enough. But if we're going to survive this, maybe it's time you stopped pretending you're not scared."

Lira glanced at him briefly, her expression unreadable. Then she turned back to the path, her voice steady but low. "Fear doesn't get a say in this."

Kael didn't respond, but he couldn't shake the unease crawling along his spine. The figures might have vanished, but the feeling of being watched remained, heavier than ever. As they moved deeper into the mist, the oppressive presence of Varunel pressed closer, whispering promises neither of them dared to acknowledge.

The fog seemed to tighten its grip on the city as Lira and Kael pressed forward, the oppressive silence broken only by their measured footsteps and the occasional drip of water from unseen cracks in the stone. The ruins grew denser, the remnants of buildings looming higher, their weathered facades etched with faint, intricate patterns that seemed almost deliberate.

Kael adjusted his pack and pulled out the map Elder Thorne had given them. The parchment crackled softly as he unfolded it, the symbols drawn in dark ink catching what little light filtered through the mist. He studied it for a moment, his brow furrowing.

"Lira," he called softly, breaking the stillness.

"What is it now?" she asked, not breaking stride.

"These symbols," Kael said, holding up the map. "They're… familiar."

Lira finally stopped, turning to look at him. Her tone was curt. "Familiar how?"

He gestured toward one of the crumbling walls beside them, pointing to a faint carving that curved and spiraled along the stone's surface. "Look. It's the same as this one."

Lira approached, narrowing her eyes at the symbol. It was nearly identical to one drawn on the map—an angular design intersected by flowing lines, like a star partially obscured by waves. She frowned but remained silent.

Kael tilted the map toward her. "This can't be a coincidence."

"It's an old city," she said dismissively, stepping back. "Symbols repeat."

Kael raised an eyebrow. "Sure, but this map was drawn by Thorne, right? She must've known these symbols would match something here. Maybe they're markers."

"Or just decorations," Lira replied. "We don't know what they mean."

Kael folded the map slightly, holding it at eye level. "What if they mean 'don't go this way'? Or 'danger ahead'? Lira, if this map can help us avoid walking straight into something that's going to kill us—"

"It's not a warning system," she interrupted, her voice steady but hard. "Thorne said it would lead us to answers, not keep us safe."

"Maybe it's both," Kael suggested, his tone softer. "Or maybe we're supposed to figure that out."

Lira sighed, rubbing her temple. "And you're the expert now?"

Kael shrugged, a faint grin tugging at the corner of his mouth. "I mean, I've got a map. That's more than you've got."

She shot him a sharp look, though her lips twitched slightly in what might have been the ghost of a smirk. "Fine. If you're so confident, where do we go next?"

Kael held the map up again, scanning the faint lines and symbols. "The next marker should be... there." He pointed toward an alley where the mist seemed slightly thinner, the faint outline of another carved symbol just visible on the far wall.

Lira followed his gaze, her expression skeptical. "You're basing this on a piece of parchment and some old carvings."

"And you're basing everything on stubbornness," Kael retorted. "What's the harm in following the map? Worst case, we end up where we're going anyway."

She hesitated, her hand brushing the talisman at her neck. The metal was cool to the touch, grounding her despite her growing unease. "If this leads us in circles, you're taking the blame."

"Deal," Kael said with a grin, already stepping toward the alley. "Come on, let's see where this takes us."

Lira followed reluctantly, her eyes scanning the surrounding ruins as they moved. The symbols grew more frequent, appearing on walls, archways, and even broken cobblestones. Each one seemed deliberate, their lines too precise to be mere decoration. She hated to admit it, but Kael might be onto something.

"So," Kael said after a moment, his voice lighter now that he was leading. "How's it feel to let me take the reins for once?"

"Don't get used to it," Lira replied dryly. "This is an experiment, not a promotion."

He chuckled, glancing over his shoulder at her. "You know, I think you're secretly enjoying this. Letting someone else make the decisions for a change."

"Enjoying is a stretch," she muttered, though her tone lacked its usual bite. "I just don't want to hear you whining if we miss something important."

"Fair enough," Kael said, his grin widening. "But you have to admit—this map might actually be useful."

She didn't respond immediately, her gaze lingering on another symbol etched into a doorway they passed. It matched one of the larger symbols on the map, its edges worn but still distinct. Her fingers tightened around the talisman, and for the first time, she felt a flicker of doubt—not about Kael, but about her own reluctance to trust the artifacts.

"It's a tool," she said finally. "Nothing more."

"And tools are meant to be used," Kael replied, his voice gentle but firm. "You don't have to believe in magic to see that."

They reached the end of the alley, where the mist parted slightly to reveal a small courtyard. In its center stood a broken statue, its surface weathered and covered in more of the strange carvings. Kael stopped, unfolding the map fully.

"This is it," he said, pointing to the statue. "It's marked right here. Thorne must've known we'd find this."

Lira approached cautiously, her eyes scanning the courtyard. The air felt heavier here, and the silence was almost deafening. She looked at the statue, then back at Kael.

"Let's hope you're right," she said quietly.

Kael smirked. "You know I am."

But as they stepped closer, the mist shifted again, curling inward like a living thing. Whatever lay ahead, the map was only the beginning—and Lira wasn't sure she was ready to trust it fully. Not yet.

The courtyard lay silent, the mist coiling tightly around the crumbling remnants of the city. Kael and Lira stood near the broken statue, its surface etched with symbols that seemed to shift under their gaze. The air was heavy, thick with an unspoken tension that neither of them could shake.

Then it came—a faint sound, distant and haunting. A soft laugh, almost childlike, carried on the mist like a memory surfacing from the depths of a forgotten dream.

Kael froze, his hand gripping the hilt of his blade. "Did you hear that?"

Lira's jaw tightened, her eyes scanning the empty space around them. "It's the wind."

"That wasn't the wind," Kael muttered, his voice low. "That was laughter."

"Don't start," Lira snapped, her voice sharper than intended.

Kael turned toward her, his eyes wide with unease. "You heard it too, didn't you? Don't pretend you didn't."

She didn't respond immediately, her gaze fixed on the shadows flickering at the edge of the mist. The laughter came again, closer this time, followed by something worse—an echo of their names, distorted but unmistakable.

"Lira… Kael…" The voice was soft, lilting, and utterly wrong.

Kael's breath hitched. "Okay, that's not normal."

"It's a trick," Lira said, her tone clipped as she turned sharply away from the sound. "Ignore it."

Kael stared at her, disbelief etched into his features. "Ignore it? Lira, it just said our names. You can't seriously think that's—"

"It doesn't matter what I think," she interrupted, her voice rising. "We don't stop. We don't listen. That's how this place gets to you."

Kael stepped closer, his voice softening. "Lira, come on. You're acting like this isn't affecting you. But it is, isn't it?"

She turned on him, her eyes blazing. "I don't have the luxury of being affected, Kael. One of us has to stay focused."

Kael recoiled slightly at her outburst, his expression a mix of concern and frustration. "Focused on what? Getting to the heart of this cursed city and hoping we survive?"

"Yes," she said firmly. "That's exactly what we're doing."

The laughter echoed again, louder now, bouncing off the unseen walls of the courtyard. Kael flinched, his hand tightening on his blade. "And what if we don't survive? What if this place is already—"

"Stop," Lira snapped, cutting him off. "I'm not doing this with you, Kael. We keep moving. End of discussion."

Kael exhaled slowly, his frustration giving way to a deep, simmering worry. "You think shutting everything out makes you stronger, but it doesn't. It makes you blind."

"I'm not blind," she said through gritted teeth, turning away from him. "I see this place for exactly what it is—a trap. And I'm not letting it win."

Kael hesitated, his gaze lingering on her tense shoulders. "You keep saying that. But what happens when it's not just me you're ignoring? What happens when this place gets into your head too?"

She didn't answer, her grip tightening on the talisman hanging from her neck. The cool metal was a reminder of Elder Thorne's warnings, a lifeline she refused to fully trust but couldn't bring herself to discard.

Kael took a step closer, his voice soft but insistent. "You don't have to do this alone, you know. Whatever this place is, we're in it together."

She glanced at him, her expression briefly softening before the tension returned. "Together doesn't work if one of us gives in. So don't."

Kael sighed, nodding reluctantly. "Alright. But you're not as invincible as you think, Lira."

"Good thing I don't need to be," she muttered, turning back to the path. "Let's go."

They moved forward, the mist parting slightly as they left the courtyard behind. The laughter and whispers faded, but the oppressive weight of the city remained, pressing down on them with every step. Kael stayed close, his unease growing as he watched Lira's rigid posture and clenched fists.

"You know," he said after a moment, "ignoring it doesn't make it go away."

"It keeps it from getting worse," she replied curtly.

"Does it?" Kael asked, his voice quiet. "Because from where I'm standing, it looks like it's already in your head."

She didn't respond, her pace quickening as though she could outrun the city's pull. But Kael wasn't wrong—her composure was slipping, cracks forming in the wall she'd built around herself. The voices, the laughter, the whispers—they weren't just distractions. They were reminders of something she couldn't quite place, something that felt both foreign and painfully familiar.

As they pushed deeper into the ruins, the mist thickened again, and the city's oppressive presence grew stronger. Kael stayed close, his concern for Lira outweighing his fear of the shadows around them. Whatever secrets Varunel held, it was clear they were far from finished with the two of them.

Chapter 4
Testing the Veil

The mist lay heavy over the streets of Varunel, muffling sound and casting the crumbling ruins in an eerie, muted light. Lira and Kael moved cautiously, their eyes scanning every shadow for signs of danger. The oppressive silence was broken only by the crunch of rubble underfoot and the faint hum of energy that seemed to pulse from the city itself.

Kael stopped suddenly, his gaze catching on something glinting faintly in the debris. "Wait," he said, crouching to brush away the dirt and shards of stone. "There's something here."

Lira turned, frowning as she stepped closer. "What is it?"

Kael unearthed a small, broken charm. It was roughly the size of his palm, its edges jagged and cracked, but the intricate carvings on its surface were unmistakable. They matched the design on Elder Thorne's talisman, though this piece was clearly damaged and worn.

"It's like the talisman," Kael said, holding it up. The faint light reflected off the carvings, casting strange patterns on the surrounding mist. "Look at the markings. They're almost identical."

Lira crossed her arms, her expression skeptical. "It's broken. Whatever it was, it's useless now."

Kael stood, turning the charm over in his hands. "You don't know that. This could be a clue—a piece of the puzzle. Maybe it tells us something about the talisman, or the city."

"It tells us that people left junk behind when this place fell apart," Lira said flatly. "That's all."

Kael frowned, glancing between her and the charm. "You don't actually believe that, do you? Look at this thing. It's not just some random piece of rubble. It's tied to all of this."

Lira sighed, turning away. "Even if it is, what are you planning to do with it? Wave it around and hope it magically solves all our problems?"

"I don't know," Kael admitted, his voice quiet but firm. "But I'm not just going to ignore it. Not when it could be important."

"Important how?" she asked, her tone sharp. "It's broken, Kael. It doesn't work."

Kael hesitated, his fingers brushing over the carvings again. The charm felt cold in his hands, heavier than it should have been, as if it carried a weight beyond its physical form. "Maybe it doesn't need to work. Maybe it's meant to show us something."

Lira turned back to him, her eyes narrowing. "You're grasping at straws."

"And you're refusing to see what's right in front of you," he shot back, his frustration breaking through. "Every time something like this shows up, you dismiss it. Why?"

"Because chasing after every little thing this city throws at us is how we die," she said coldly. "We stick to what we know works—the talisman, the map—and we keep moving."

Kael's jaw tightened, but he didn't argue. Instead, he slipped the broken charm into his pocket, his expression hardening. "Fine. But I'm keeping it. Just in case."

Lira shook her head, her voice laced with irritation. "Do whatever you want. Just don't let it distract you."

They continued walking, the tension between them thick in the air. The mist seemed to close in tighter, the faint hum of energy growing stronger with each step. Lira's eyes darted toward Kael as he walked slightly ahead, his hand brushing against his pocket where the charm rested.

She hated to admit it, even to herself, but something about the charm unsettled her. Its design was too similar to the talisman to be a coincidence, and its presence raised questions she didn't want to dwell on. Questions about the city, about the artifacts they carried, and about how much of this journey was truly within their control.

"Kael," she said after a long silence, her voice softer. "Just… be careful with that thing. We don't know what it might do."

Kael glanced back at her, surprised by her change in tone. "I will," he said, his voice quieter now. "But you should trust me, Lira. Not everything here is out to get us."

She didn't respond, her gaze fixed on the path ahead. The shadows shifted in the mist, flickering along the edges of the ruins like ghostly echoes. The city seemed to watch, its presence more oppressive than ever.

And as they moved deeper into Varunel, the broken charm felt heavier in Kael's pocket, as if waiting for its moment to reveal its secrets.

The mist clung to them like a second skin, dense and almost suffocating. The oppressive silence was broken only by Kael's insistent voice.

"Lira, we need to try it," he said, pulling the broken charm from his pocket and holding it up for her to see. Its cracked surface glinted faintly, the carvings catching what little light penetrated the fog.

Lira didn't stop walking, her voice clipped as she replied. "We already have a working talisman. Why waste time with something that's broken?"

Kael quickened his pace, moving to step in front of her. "Because we don't know what it can do. It's worth finding out."

She shot him a sharp glare, her hand brushing the hilt of her blade. "What if it does nothing? Or worse, what if it makes things harder? We don't have the luxury of playing around."

"This isn't playing around," Kael said, his tone rising. "This is trying to understand the tools we have. What if this charm can do something the talisman can't?"

"Like what?" she snapped. "It's broken, Kael. Whatever power it had is gone."

"Then let's prove it," Kael said, stepping back and holding the charm out in front of him. "If it's useless, fine. But if it works, even a little, that's something."

Lira hesitated, her frustration visible in the tight line of her jaw. "Fine," she said reluctantly. "But if this gets us killed, I'm holding you responsible."

Kael didn't respond, his focus entirely on the charm. He held it higher, turning it toward the swirling mist ahead. For a moment, nothing happened. Then, the mist seemed to ripple, as though reacting to an unseen force. It didn't part entirely, but it shifted slightly, creating a faint, narrow path.

"Did you see that?" Kael asked, his voice tinged with excitement.

Lira folded her arms, unimpressed. "It's not exactly groundbreaking. The talisman does more, and we know it works."

Kael frowned, lowering the charm slightly. The mist crept back in almost immediately, the path disappearing as quickly as it had formed. "But this means it's not useless," he insisted. "It's connected to the city somehow."

"Everything here is connected to the city," Lira said, her tone exasperated. "The mist, the whispers, the shadows. That doesn't mean we can trust it."

Kael stepped closer to her, holding up the charm again. "I'm not saying we trust it. I'm saying we use it. What if this is another key, like the talisman? What if it can help us get through the city?"

Lira sighed, rubbing her temples. "Or what if it's bait? Something left behind to lure people deeper into Varunel."

"Then we're already doing exactly what it wants," Kael shot back. "We're here, aren't we? The city's already got us. At least this gives us something to work with."

She eyed the charm warily, her voice softening slightly. "And what happens when it stops working? Or worse, when it turns against us?"

Kael hesitated, his grip on the charm tightening. "Then we deal with it. But we can't just ignore it because we're afraid of what might happen."

Lira shook her head, her gaze hard. "I'm not afraid, Kael. I'm cautious. There's a difference."

"Sometimes there isn't," Kael muttered, his voice quiet but pointed. He held the charm up again, watching the mist ripple faintly in response. "This thing is trying to tell us something. I don't know what, but I'm not throwing it away without finding out."

Lira stared at him for a long moment, her expression unreadable. Finally, she let out a slow breath. "Fine. Keep your charm. But don't get too comfortable with it. The last thing we need is for you to start trusting something we don't understand."

Kael smiled faintly, slipping the charm back into his pocket. "I'm not trusting it. I'm trying to understand it. There's a difference."

"Not much of one," she muttered, turning back toward the path. "Let's go. If we waste any more time here, we won't need the charm to get us killed."

Kael followed, his hand brushing the charm in his pocket as they moved forward. The mist seemed to close in around them again, the faint ripple gone as though it had never been. But Kael couldn't shake the feeling that the charm was watching, waiting for its moment.

And as they pressed deeper into the city, the divide between Lira's skepticism and Kael's curiosity felt like a shadow trailing just behind them, ready to strike.

The mist seemed thicker now, curling tighter around them as if the city itself was listening. Lira walked ahead, her steps brisk and deliberate, her hand resting on the hilt of her blade. Kael trailed behind, the broken charm weighing heavily in his pocket. The silence between them was suffocating, each caught in the aftermath of their argument.

"You didn't have to shut me down back there," Kael finally said, his voice breaking the heavy silence.

Lira didn't turn, her voice clipped. "I didn't shut you down. I pointed out the risks."

"You dismissed it," he countered, his tone edged with frustration. "Like everything else that doesn't fit into your plan."

She stopped abruptly, spinning to face him, her gaze sharp. "My plan is to get us out of here alive. That's all that matters."

Kael held her stare, his jaw tightening. "And you think ignoring everything we don't understand is the way to do that?"

"I think staying focused is the way to do that," she shot back. "This city is designed to distract us. The second we start chasing every mystery it throws our way, we're dead."

Kael exhaled sharply, shaking his head. "It's not just a mystery, Lira. That charm—whatever it is—it's connected to all of this. Maybe if you'd just—"

"Enough," she interrupted, her tone sharp. "I don't have time to argue about a broken trinket."

Kael clenched his fists, biting back a retort. The tension between them hung thick in the air, heavier than the mist. After a long moment, Lira turned and started walking again, her shoulders stiff.

As they continued deeper into the ruins, the whispers began to creep back, faint at first but steadily growing louder. The disjointed syllables wound through the air like smoke, curling into incomprehensible fragments of speech. Kael tried to ignore them, but something about their tone felt different this time—more direct, more personal.

He stopped in his tracks, his head tilting slightly as he strained to listen. Among the garbled voices, one stood out, clearer than the rest. "Kael…" He stiffened, his heart pounding. The voice wasn't just a sound; it was a presence, brushing against the edges of his mind like a cold breath.

"Lira," he called, his voice unsteady. "Do you hear that?"

She glanced back at him, her expression unreadable. "I hear whispers, same as always. What is it?"

"It… it said my name," Kael said, his eyes darting into the fog. "It's talking to me."

"It's not talking to you," she said firmly, stepping closer. "It's manipulating you. That's what this place does."

"You don't understand," he said, his voice rising slightly. "This is different. It's not just noise. It's—" He broke off, his hand moving to the charm in his pocket.

Lira's eyes flicked to his hand, her expression tightening. "Kael. Don't."

"I'm not doing anything," he snapped, his frustration boiling over. "I'm just trying to figure out what's going on."

"What's going on," she said coldly, "is that this city is getting to you. You need to shut it out."

"And you need to stop pretending you're immune to it," he shot back, his voice sharp. "I've seen how it affects you, Lira. You can't just keep ignoring it."

Her jaw tightened, but she didn't respond. Instead, she turned away, her focus fixed on the path ahead. The whispers grew louder, their tone shifting again, becoming almost taunting. "Kael…" the voice called again, softer now, almost familiar.

He flinched, his hand tightening around the charm. "It knows me," he muttered under his breath. "How does it know me?"

Lira stopped and turned to face him, her gaze hard. "It doesn't. It knows how to make you think it does. That's the point. Don't let it win."

Kael stared at her, his frustration giving way to something closer to fear. "What if it's not just a trick? What if it's trying to tell me something?"

"What if it's trying to lead you off a cliff?" she countered, her voice sharp. "We don't have the luxury of playing 'what if,' Kael. We stick to what we know. That's the only way we survive."

Her words hung in the air, cutting through the whispers like a blade. Kael exhaled shakily, his grip on the charm loosening. "Fine," he said quietly. "But that doesn't mean I'm ignoring it."

"Just don't let it control you," she said, her tone softening slightly. "That's when it wins."

He nodded reluctantly, falling back into step beside her. But as they moved forward, the whispers lingered at the edges of his mind, their words threading into his thoughts like poison. And though Lira didn't say anything more, the tight set of her shoulders betrayed the weight she was carrying—the fear she refused to acknowledge.

The city seemed to pulse around them, its energy pressing closer with each step. Shadows flickered in the mist, moving just out of reach. Kael tried to shake off the feeling of being watched, but the sensation gnawed at him, sharpening his unease.

Finally, Lira broke the silence, her voice low. "We're getting close to something. I can feel it."

Kael glanced at her, his expression skeptical. "Feel it? Or hear it?"

"Both," she admitted, her tone grudging. "But it doesn't matter. Whatever's ahead, we're not turning back."

He let out a humorless laugh. "Would you ever?"

"No," she said simply, her voice steady. "And neither would you."

The mist thickened, swirling around them in slow, deliberate eddies that seemed to respond to their every movement. The ruins loomed higher on either side of the path, their jagged edges like teeth threatening to swallow them whole. The whispers had receded into an eerie silence, but the oppressive weight of Varunel's presence was palpable, pressing down on Lira and Kael with every step.

Lira slowed as the path narrowed, her hand instinctively tightening on the hilt of her blade. "This place doesn't want us here," she said, her voice low but resolute.

"Does it ever?" Kael muttered, his gaze darting around the shifting fog. He still held the broken charm in his pocket, its jagged surface pressing against his palm like a lifeline. The air felt different here—heavier, charged with something unnameable.

As they stepped forward, the mist seemed to condense ahead of them, its swirling tendrils twisting and darkening until they formed the shape of a figure. It was faint, barely more than a shadow, but unmistakable in its humanlike outline. The figure raised an arm, its hand—or what passed for one—pointing toward a narrow alley to their left.

Kael froze, his breath catching. "Do you see that?" he asked, his voice hushed.

Lira nodded, her expression hardening. "I see it."

"It's… showing us the way," Kael said, stepping closer. His voice held a strange mixture of awe and apprehension. "Maybe it's trying to help."

"Or maybe it's leading us into a trap," Lira replied sharply, reaching out to grab his arm before he could get too close. "We don't follow shadows."

Kael turned to her, his brows furrowing. "What if this is part of the city's curse? What if it's trying to guide us, not hurt us?"

"What if it's both?" Lira countered, her tone cold but steady. "What if it's guiding us somewhere we don't want to go?"

Kael hesitated, glancing back at the figure. The shadow remained still, its form flickering slightly but its gesture unwavering. The alley it pointed to was narrow and dark, the ruins on either side leaning inward as though trying to close it off entirely.

"This place doesn't do anything for free," Lira continued, her voice quieter now. "Everything here has a price, Kael. Don't forget that."

He didn't respond immediately, his gaze fixed on the shadow. "We don't have many options," he said finally. "If it wanted to kill us, it's had plenty of chances. What if this is the only way forward?"

Lira exhaled sharply, her grip tightening on her blade. "If we follow it, we stay alert. The second it feels wrong, we turn back."

Kael nodded, his fingers brushing the charm in his pocket. "Agreed."

They stepped toward the alley, the mist parting slightly as they moved. The shadow faded as they neared it, dissolving into the fog like smoke on the wind. The alley itself was narrow, its walls covered in faint, glowing symbols that pulsed with a dull, rhythmic light. The air was colder here, and the oppressive energy of the city seemed to close in even tighter.

Lira led the way, her steps slow and deliberate. She scanned every inch of the path ahead, her senses on high alert. Kael followed close behind, his grip on the charm tightening with every step.

"This doesn't feel right," Lira muttered, her voice barely audible over the low hum emanating from the walls.

"It doesn't feel wrong, either," Kael replied, though his tone lacked confidence. "Not yet."

The alley twisted sharply, the walls narrowing even further until it felt like they were being funneled toward something. The light from the symbols grew brighter, their pulsing rhythm faster. Lira stopped abruptly, holding up a hand to signal Kael to halt.

"There's something ahead," she said, her voice tense.

Kael peered over her shoulder, his eyes narrowing as he tried to make out the shape in the distance. The mist was thicker here, clinging to the walls and floor like a living thing. He thought he saw movement—a flicker of shadow or light—but it was gone before he could be sure.

"What do you think it is?" he asked quietly.

"Nothing good," she replied. "Stay close."

They moved forward again, the air growing colder with each step. The tension between them was almost tangible, the weight of their unspoken fears pressing down like a physical force. Lira's grip on her blade tightened, her knuckles white, while Kael's thoughts churned with questions he couldn't answer.

As they reached the end of the alley, the mist parted slightly, revealing a circular clearing surrounded by crumbling walls. At the center stood a pedestal, its surface etched with symbols similar to those on the talisman and the charm. The air hummed with energy, the sound resonating in their chests.

Lira stopped, her eyes narrowing as she studied the clearing. "This is it," she said quietly. "Whatever's waiting for us—it's here."

Kael didn't respond, his gaze fixed on the pedestal. The charm in his pocket grew warmer, almost as if it were reacting to the energy in the clearing. He swallowed hard, his heart pounding as he took a cautious step forward.

The city's grip tightened around them, its presence more oppressive than ever. And though neither of them said it aloud, they both knew there was no turning back now.

Chapter 5
Echoes of the Past

The mist shifted, thinning slightly, revealing fragments of Varunel's past etched into the ruins around them. The air seemed heavier, laden with something unseen yet palpable. Kael and Lira slowed as faint figures emerged from the fog—ghostly shapes that flickered like shadows on water.

Kael stopped first, his breath catching. "Lira, look," he said softly, gesturing ahead.

Lira stepped closer, her hand instinctively resting on her blade. "What now?" she muttered, her tone edged with weariness.

"Over there," Kael said, nodding toward a small clearing where the apparition of a child played. The child was laughing, running in circles with arms outstretched, as if chasing something unseen. The sound was faint, barely audible, but unmistakably joyful.

Kael's expression softened, his voice filled with wonder. "She's just a kid."

Lira frowned, her eyes narrowing as she scanned the vision. "She's not real."

"You don't know that," Kael said, stepping closer. "What if she was? What if this is... I don't know, some part of her still here?"

Lira grabbed his arm, stopping him. "Don't," she said firmly. "It's not her. It's this place. Don't let it pull you in."

Kael hesitated, his gaze lingering on the child. "But look at her. She's so... happy. How can that be dangerous?"

"Because that's exactly what it wants you to think," Lira snapped. "This city doesn't show us anything for no reason. It's trying to mess with your head."

Kael turned to her, frustration flickering in his eyes. "Or maybe it's showing us the truth. Have you ever considered that? That not everything here is out to hurt us?"

Lira's jaw tightened, her voice low and cold. "No. Because everything here *is* out to hurt us. Don't forget that."

Before Kael could respond, another vision appeared—a translucent image of an elderly couple walking arm-in-arm through the mist. They moved slowly, their steps steady and deliberate, their faces serene. The man leaned slightly on a cane, while the woman looked up at him with a soft smile.

Kael's breath hitched. "They're... so peaceful. Like they don't even notice the city around them."

"Or like they're part of it," Lira said, her tone cutting. She turned away, refusing to look at the figures for longer than a moment.

Kael glanced at her, his frustration mounting. "Why do you always do that?"

"Do what?" she shot back, her eyes narrowing.

"Act like nothing here matters," he said, his voice rising slightly. "Like everything is just another trap."

"Because it is," she said flatly. "You think these visions are here to comfort us? To make us feel better about where we are? They're not. They're here to distract us."

Kael gestured toward the elderly couple, his tone filled with emotion. "And what if they're not? What if they're just... memories? People who lived here, who were happy here. Does that scare you so much?"

"What scares me," Lira said, stepping closer, her voice low and tense, "is that you're so caught up in your feelings that you'll forget why we're here. This city doesn't want to be understood, Kael. It wants to consume us."

"And what if understanding it is the only way to survive?" Kael countered, his voice firm. "What if we're supposed to pay attention to this stuff instead of running from it?"

Lira's eyes flashed with anger. "You think stopping to watch ghosts is going to help us? You think that's what's going to get us out of here alive?"

"I think ignoring everything you don't like isn't helping either," Kael shot back. "You can't just shut it all out, Lira. Not everything is an enemy."

"Here, it is," she said coldly. "If you don't figure that out soon, you won't make it out."

Kael shook his head, stepping back slightly. "Maybe that's the difference between us. You think survival is the only thing that matters. But if we lose everything that makes us human in the process, what's the point?"

Lira froze, his words hitting her harder than she expected. For a moment, her expression softened, but the mask of cold determination quickly returned. "The point," she said quietly, "is that we're still breathing. And I intend to keep it that way."

Kael didn't respond immediately, his gaze shifting back to the figures. The elderly couple faded into the mist, their outlines dissolving like smoke. The child's laughter grew fainter until it, too, was gone, leaving only silence and the weight of their unspoken tension.

Finally, Kael let out a heavy sigh, his voice quieter now. "You don't even believe half the things you say, do you?"

Lira didn't answer. Instead, she turned and started walking again, her shoulders rigid. Kael followed, his frustration simmering just beneath the surface. The echoes of the visions lingered in his mind, their presence haunting and unshakable.

As they moved deeper into the city, the fog closed in around them once more, and the whispers began to return, faint and insistent. The memories of Varunel weren't just haunting the ruins—they were haunting them. And though Kael couldn't stop thinking about what they'd seen, Lira refused to look back.

The mist seemed to grow heavier with every step, as if Varunel itself were closing in around them. Kael walked in silence, his thoughts churning after the visions they had seen. The child's laughter, the peaceful presence of the elderly couple—these images lingered in his mind, pressing on him like a weight he couldn't shake.

"Lira," he said finally, breaking the oppressive quiet.

"What?" she replied curtly, her eyes fixed on the path ahead.

Kael hesitated, his grip tightening on the strap of his pack. "Those visions... they weren't random. There's something about this place—something it's trying to show us."

"Or something it's trying to trick us with," she said without looking back. Her tone was flat, almost mechanical.

"No," Kael said firmly, stepping closer to her side. "It wasn't just tricks. That child, that couple—they weren't threats. They were memories. Pieces of the people who lived here."

Lira's jaw tightened, but she didn't respond.

Kael pressed on, his voice growing more insistent. "What if that's part of the curse? What if Varunel traps people here—not just their bodies, but their souls? What if those people can't leave, even after—"

"Stop," Lira interrupted, turning to face him. Her expression was hard, her eyes sharp. "Don't do this."

"Do what?" Kael asked, frustration creeping into his voice.

"Turn this into something bigger than it is," she said, her tone icy. "This city isn't some tragic, haunted place. It's a trap. That's all. You start thinking it's more than that, and you'll lose focus."

Kael stared at her, disbelief flickering in his eyes. "So you think those visions meant nothing? That those people didn't mean anything?"

"They're not people," Lira snapped. "Not anymore. They're bait. This place will show you whatever it needs to in order to make you hesitate. Don't let it."

"You don't know that," Kael argued. "What if they're still here, somehow? What if they're trying to reach us, to warn us?"

"And what if that's exactly what Varunel wants you to think?" she shot back. "What if the second you start listening, it's already too late?"

Kael shook his head, his voice rising. "Not everything is a trap, Lira. Maybe this city is more than just some cursed ruin. Maybe it's... alive, in a way. And maybe those people are still part of it."

"Alive?" Lira scoffed, her tone dripping with sarcasm. "You think Varunel is alive? That it's just misunderstood?"

"I think there's more going on here than you're willing to admit," Kael said, his voice steady despite her mockery. "And if we ignore it, we're never going to understand what we're up against."

"What we're up against," she said sharply, stepping closer to him, "is a city designed to kill anyone foolish enough to come here. You want to waste time feeling sorry for ghosts? Fine. But don't drag me into it."

Kael's frustration boiled over, his voice rising. "Why are you like this? Why can't you just admit that this place is getting to you, too? That maybe, just maybe, you don't have all the answers?"

Lira's eyes flashed with anger, but there was something else there, too—something she quickly buried. "Because if I let this place get to me, we're dead," she said, her voice low and hard. "Is that what you want, Kael? For both of us to fall apart?"

"That's not what I'm saying," Kael replied, his tone softening slightly. "I'm saying we can't just ignore what's happening here. If we don't try to understand it, how do we fight it?"

Lira let out a harsh breath, turning away. "You fight it by surviving. That's all that matters."

Kael watched her for a long moment, his frustration giving way to something closer to sadness. "You really believe that, don't you? That surviving is the only thing that matters."

She didn't respond, her focus fixed on the mist ahead. Her silence was answer enough.

Kael sighed, running a hand through his hair. "Maybe that's why this place hasn't broken you yet. Because you don't let yourself feel anything."

Lira froze, her back to him. Her hand drifted to the talisman at her neck, her fingers brushing the cold metal as if seeking reassurance. "Feeling doesn't keep you alive," she said quietly, almost to herself.

"And shutting everything out doesn't make you stronger," Kael replied, his voice gentle now. "It just makes you alone."

She didn't turn, didn't speak. For a moment, the silence between them was deafening, filled with all the things neither of them wanted to say.

Finally, Lira started walking again, her steps brisk and deliberate. Kael followed, his thoughts churning. The visions, the whispers, the feeling that Varunel was alive in some terrible way—all of it pressed on him like a weight he couldn't shake. But Lira's refusal to acknowledge it made that weight even heavier.

As they moved deeper into the city, the mist seemed to close in tighter, the air growing colder. And though neither of them spoke again, the tension between them was thicker than ever, their opposing beliefs driving a wedge deeper into their fragile alliance.

The mist grew heavier, clinging to the ruins like a living shroud. Lira's steps slowed as the oppressive silence settled over them. Kael followed a few paces behind, his attention flickering between her and the swirling fog. The tension between them lingered, their earlier argument still fresh, but the city had a way of making even the sharpest conflicts feel distant under its weight.

Then, ahead of them, the mist began to shift. A faint figure emerged from the fog, its edges blurry and indistinct. Lira stopped abruptly, her breath catching as the form solidified. It was a woman—tall, with a familiar stride and an air of quiet authority. She was draped in a tattered cloak, her face partially obscured by the mist, but the sharp lines of her jaw and the confident tilt of her head were unmistakable.

Lira's grip tightened on the hilt of her blade, her knuckles white. Her voice was barely above a whisper. "No."

Kael stepped up beside her, frowning. "What is it? What do you see?"

"It's nothing," she snapped, her voice sharp but trembling. "Keep moving."

Kael's gaze shifted to the apparition. He couldn't make out the details, but the figure radiated a quiet power, standing unnervingly still in the mist. "That doesn't look like nothing," he said, his tone cautious. "Who is she?"

"She's no one," Lira said, her jaw tightening. "Just another trick."

Kael studied her, noticing the way her hand trembled slightly at her side. "You know her," he said quietly. "Don't you?"

"No," Lira said firmly, but her voice wavered. She turned away, her steps brisk as she moved forward. "It's just the city messing with us again. Don't fall for it."

Kael hesitated, glancing back at the figure. The apparition didn't move, but its presence lingered like a shadow in his mind. He jogged to catch up with Lira, his tone soft but insistent. "You recognized her, Lira. I could see it."

Lira didn't look at him, her gaze fixed ahead. "You're imagining things."

"No, I'm not," Kael said, stepping in front of her to block her path. "You froze back there. You never freeze."

"I said it's nothing," she snapped, her voice rising. "Drop it."

Kael didn't budge, his eyes searching hers. "You can't keep doing this. Pretending like none of this affects you. It's not weakness to feel something, Lira."

Her jaw clenched, and she took a step back, her posture rigid. "Feel something? About what? A ghost? A shadow? It's not real, Kael. None of it is."

"Then why are you shaking?" he asked quietly.

"I'm not shaking," she said, though her voice betrayed her. She turned sharply, trying to move past him, but Kael grabbed her arm, his grip firm but not unkind.

"Lira," he said, his tone softer now. "Who was she?"

Lira froze, her eyes narrowing as she glared at him. For a moment, she seemed ready to lash out, but then something shifted in her expression—an emotion she quickly buried. She yanked her arm free, her voice cold. "It doesn't matter."

"It does matter," Kael said, his voice rising slightly. "You've been acting like this city hasn't gotten to you, like you're untouchable. But it's not true, is it? It's in your head, just like it's in mine."

Lira let out a harsh laugh, shaking her head. "You think I'm scared? That I'm falling apart because I saw some ghost that looks like someone I used to know? Grow up, Kael. That's exactly what this place wants."

"Maybe it's not about fear," Kael said, his tone steady despite her anger. "Maybe it's showing you something you need to face. Something you've been running from."

She stiffened, her gaze flickering toward the mist behind him. The figure was gone, but its presence lingered, an echo in her mind. Her voice was quieter now, though no less sharp. "This city doesn't want us to face anything. It wants to break us. That's all it is. Don't make it something it's not."

Kael hesitated, watching her carefully. "And what if you're wrong? What if it's not just trying to break us? What if it's trying to show us the truth?"

Lira's eyes flashed with anger, but there was something else there too—fear, buried deep beneath the surface. She turned away, her voice low. "The truth doesn't matter if we don't survive."

Kael stepped closer, his voice soft. "And what if surviving means facing it?"

She didn't respond, her fingers brushing the talisman at her neck as if seeking strength. Her shoulders were rigid, her movements deliberate as she started walking again.

Kael followed in silence, his thoughts swirling. The tension between them hung heavy in the air, a fragile thread threatening to snap. He didn't press her further, but he couldn't shake the feeling that the figure in the mist had been more than just another trick of the city. It had touched something raw in Lira, something she wasn't ready to face.

As the mist closed in around them again, the whispers began to return, faint and insistent. Lira's steps quickened, her silence a shield, but Kael couldn't help but wonder how much longer she could keep the walls around her heart from crumbling.

The oppressive fog seemed thicker now, muffling even the sound of their footsteps as Lira and Kael pushed forward. The silence between them was heavy, laced with the tension that had been building since the apparition. Lira walked ahead, her movements deliberate and focused, while Kael trailed slightly behind, his expression clouded with frustration.

Finally, Kael broke the silence. "You can't keep pretending none of this is happening."

Lira didn't stop, her voice cold and clipped. "I don't have time to entertain your theories, Kael."

"It's not a theory," he shot back, quickening his pace to fall in line with her. "It's what's right in front of us. The city is getting to you, whether you admit it or not."

"I'm fine," she said sharply, her tone brooking no argument. Her gaze remained fixed ahead, scanning the ruins for any sign of movement.

"No, you're not," Kael said, his frustration bubbling to the surface. "You froze back there, Lira. You froze because you saw her."

Lira's jaw tightened, but she didn't respond.

Kael pressed on, his voice rising slightly. "You're so busy pretending you're untouchable that you can't even admit when something gets to you. You think that makes you strong?"

"It keeps me alive," she snapped, finally stopping to face him. Her eyes were hard, her stance rigid. "And it'll keep you alive, too, if you stop wasting time chasing ghosts."

Kael shook his head, exhaling sharply. "That's not strength, Lira. That's fear. You're so afraid of feeling anything, of letting this place get to you, that you're shutting everything out."

"And you're so afraid of the unknown that you'll believe anything this city shows you," she countered, her voice low but biting. "You think every shadow, every whisper is some profound message. It's not. It's a trap."

Kael's hands clenched into fists at his sides. "Maybe it is. But at least I'm willing to acknowledge what's happening instead of running from it."

"Running from it?" she echoed, her voice rising. "I'm the one keeping us moving, keeping us alive. You're the one stopping every five minutes to talk about feelings."

"This isn't about feelings," Kael said, his tone sharp. "It's about survival. And survival means understanding what we're dealing with—not pretending it doesn't exist."

Lira's gaze didn't waver, but something flickered in her expression—an emotion she quickly buried. "You think I don't understand what we're dealing with? I understand it better than you ever will."

"Then act like it," Kael said, his voice quieter now, but no less firm. "Stop pretending you're invincible. Stop shutting me out."

"I'm not shutting you out," she said, her voice colder than before. "I'm keeping us alive."

"At what cost?" Kael asked, his voice soft but laced with bitterness. "You think survival is all that matters, but you're losing yourself in the process. And you're dragging me down with you."

Her eyes narrowed, but she didn't respond immediately. When she finally spoke, her tone was icy. "If you think I'm dragging you down, then maybe you shouldn't be here."

Kael stared at her, stunned into silence for a moment. He let out a bitter laugh, shaking his head. "Is that what you really want? For me to leave? Because I'm the only one here trying to have your back."

Lira's expression hardened, her voice quiet but cutting. "I don't need anyone to have my back."

Kael stepped closer, his frustration giving way to something closer to pain. "That's your problem, Lira. You think you don't need anyone. You think shutting everyone out is the only way to survive. But it's not."

"And you think opening up, feeling things, is going to save us?" she said, her tone mocking. "You think that's what's going to keep us alive?"

Kael didn't flinch. "I think it's what makes us human. And if we lose that, then what's the point of surviving?"

For a moment, the silence between them was deafening. Lira's jaw tightened, her hand brushing the hilt of her blade as if grounding herself. Her eyes flicked away, refusing to meet his.

"Believe whatever you want," she said finally, her voice cold. "But I'm not stopping. If you want to stay behind, go ahead."

Kael's jaw tightened, his hand brushing against the broken charm in his pocket. "I'm not staying behind," he said quietly. "But don't think for a second that I'm okay with how you're handling this."

Lira didn't respond. She turned and started walking again, her steps brisk and deliberate. Kael followed, the space between them feeling wider than ever, despite the oppressive closeness of the mist.

The city seemed to press down on them, its whispers returning faintly at the edges of their awareness. Kael's frustration simmered, mingling with a growing sense of unease. He glanced at Lira, her posture rigid, her focus unwavering.

For the first time since they entered Varunel, Kael wondered if they would make it out together—or if the city would tear them apart before they reached its heart.

Chapter 6
The Heart of Varunel

The crumbling plaza at the center of Varunel stretched out before them, framed by broken arches and jagged remnants of stone. The mist was thinner here, allowing glimpses of the vast ruin, but the clarity did little to ease the tension pressing down on them. The whispers that had followed them throughout the city were louder now, rising and falling like waves. Faint cries and broken screams wove through the air, haunting and dissonant.

Kael stopped at the edge of the plaza, his breath catching in his throat. "This... this is it," he said, his voice unsteady. "The heart of Varunel."

Lira stood beside him, her hand resting lightly on the hilt of her blade. Her gaze swept across the plaza, sharp and focused. "Looks like it."

Kael turned to her, frowning. "That's all you have to say? 'Looks like it'? You don't feel that?"

"Feel what?" she asked, though her voice was tighter than usual.

"The weight," he said, gesturing vaguely at the space around them. "It's like the air is heavier here. Like the city itself is watching us."

Lira's jaw tightened, but she didn't look at him. "We knew it would be worse the closer we got. This isn't a surprise."

"It's not just worse," Kael said, his tone rising slightly. "It's... alive. It's not just whispers anymore. Do you hear them? The screams?"

"I hear them," she said curtly, her gaze scanning the plaza. "And they're nothing new. Stay focused."

Kael let out a sharp breath, his frustration bubbling to the surface. "How can you just brush it off like that? Lira, we're standing in the middle of a cursed city, listening to voices that shouldn't exist, and you're acting like it's just another day."

"Because it is just another day," she snapped, finally turning to face him. "This place has been like this since we stepped inside. Why are you acting surprised?"

"Because this is different," he said, his voice shaking. "It's not just the city anymore. It's... it's in my head. I can feel it."

Lira's expression softened slightly, but only for a moment. "That's exactly why you need to shut it out. Letting it get to you is how it wins."

Kael stared at her, his frustration giving way to something closer to desperation. "You keep saying that, like it's so easy. But it's not, Lira. You don't feel it the way I do."

"Don't I?" she asked, her voice quiet but cutting. "You think you're the only one this place is trying to break? The only one it's whispering to?"

"You don't act like it's affecting you," he said, his tone bitter. "You act like you're untouchable. Like none of this matters."

"Because I don't have the luxury of letting it matter," she said sharply. "If I fall apart, we both die. So no, I don't sit around and talk about how heavy the air feels or how loud the whispers are. I keep moving."

Kael's gaze searched hers, his voice softening. "But at what cost? You're shutting everything out, Lira. You're shutting me out."

She didn't respond immediately, her eyes flicking back to the plaza. The whispers swelled again, rising into a crescendo of faint screams that seemed to pierce the air. Her fingers tightened around her blade.

"This isn't about me," she said finally, her voice low and firm. "It's about getting through this. And we're not going to do that if you let this place get in your head."

Kael exhaled sharply, running a hand through his hair. "You keep saying that, but it's already in my head, Lira. It's been in my head since we got here."

"Then push it out," she said, her tone brooking no argument. "Don't listen to it. Don't think about it. Just focus on what's real."

"And what is real, Lira?" he asked, his voice breaking slightly. "Because standing here, I don't know anymore. I don't know if these whispers are real, or if the screams are real, or if I'm losing my mind."

She turned to him, her expression hard but her voice quieter. "What's real is us. What's real is the mission. Everything else is just noise."

Kael shook his head, his gaze dropping. "You make it sound so simple."

"It's not simple," she said, her voice softening just slightly. "But it's all we have."

The silence stretched between them, heavy and oppressive, broken only by the distant echoes of the whispers. Kael looked out over the plaza again, his shoulders slumping slightly. "This place... it's worse than I imagined."

"It's exactly what I imagined," Lira said, her tone colder again. "Now let's keep moving."

Kael hesitated, glancing at her. "Do you ever let yourself feel it? Even for a second?"

She didn't answer, her eyes fixed on the path ahead. The set of her jaw and the tight grip on her blade were the only hints that the city was wearing on her as well. Without waiting for his response, she started walking again, her steps brisk and deliberate.

Kael followed reluctantly, his thoughts churning. The whispers seemed louder now, their cries echoing in his mind like a haunting refrain. He tried to focus on Lira's steady form ahead of him, but the weight of the city pressed down harder with every step.

Varunel's heart loomed closer, and with it, the promise of answers—or destruction.

The mist swirled heavily around them as Kael paused, pulling out the map they'd been given by Elder Thorne. The edges of the parchment felt damp from the humidity, and the intricate symbols drawn across its surface seemed to shift under his gaze. At first, he thought it was just a trick of the dim light, but as he tilted the map toward the faint glow of the talisman hanging around Lira's neck, he realized something was changing.

"Lira," he called softly, his voice cutting through the oppressive silence. "Look at this."

Lira glanced back at him, her brow furrowing in irritation. "What now? We need to keep moving."

"No, wait," Kael insisted, stepping closer to show her the map. "The symbols... they're moving."

She frowned, peering over his shoulder at the parchment. At first, it looked the same—lines and symbols drawn in precise, ancient patterns. But as she stared, she noticed it too: the faint, almost imperceptible shifting of the symbols. They glided across the map like rivers redirecting their course, slowly settling into new positions that seemed to form a path.

"What the hell?" Lira muttered, her voice low.

"It's reacting to the city," Kael said, his tone filled with a mixture of wonder and apprehension. "It's showing us where to go."

"Or leading us straight into a trap," Lira replied sharply, crossing her arms. "You're so quick to trust anything that looks like guidance."

Kael met her gaze, his tone firm. "I'm not trusting it blindly, but we can't ignore this. The map hasn't done anything like this before. It's connected to the city somehow—just like the talisman, just like everything else."

Lira hesitated, glancing between him and the map. The faint glow from the talisman caught her eye, its light pulsing softly in time with the shifting symbols. "And what if it's leading us straight into the heart of whatever curse this place holds?" she asked, her tone quieter now. "Have you thought of that?"

"Yes," Kael said simply. "But we don't have another choice. If we don't follow it, we're just wandering blind."

Lira's lips pressed into a thin line, her hand instinctively brushing against the hilt of her blade. She didn't like it—didn't like relying on something she didn't fully understand. But the weight of the city's presence pressed down on her, a constant reminder that their time was running out. Slowly, she nodded.

"Fine," she said, her voice clipped. "We'll follow it. But the second it feels wrong, we stop."

Kael nodded, relief flickering across his face. "Agreed."

He adjusted the map in his hands, watching as the symbols finally settled into a clear pattern. The path they formed wound through the ruins like a labyrinth, leading toward a central point marked by an ominous cluster of swirling shapes. Kael's grip tightened on the map as he turned to Lira.

"It's leading us there," he said, pointing to the center of the map.

Lira glanced at the marked location, her expression hardening. "Of course it is. Straight into the heart of the city."

"That's where the answers will be," Kael said, though there was a note of uncertainty in his voice.

"Or where we'll die," Lira muttered under her breath. She adjusted the talisman around her neck, the glow steadying her nerves as she turned back toward the path. "Let's move."

As they started forward, the air around them seemed to shift. The mist parted slightly, just enough to reveal faint outlines of the ruins ahead, as though the city itself were guiding their way. The symbols on the map continued to glow faintly, pulsing in rhythm with their steps.

Kael watched the shifting light with a mix of awe and caution. "Do you think it's alive?" he asked after a long silence.

"What?" Lira asked, glancing at him over her shoulder.

"The city," Kael said. "Do you think it's alive? That it's... aware of us?"

Lira didn't answer immediately, her gaze fixed ahead. Finally, she said, "If it is, it hasn't done anything to prove it's on our side."

Kael nodded, his thoughts churning as they followed the glowing path marked on the map. The ruins seemed to grow taller around them, the air colder, heavier. The whispers were quieter now, but their absence was almost more unsettling than their presence.

For the first time, Kael noticed Lira stealing glances at the map as they walked. Her stoicism hadn't faltered, but the faint lines of tension around her mouth betrayed her unease. She didn't trust the map—or the city—but she was following them anyway. It was a small shift, but it marked a turning point.

Kael didn't press her further, sensing that pushing too hard might shatter the fragile understanding between them. Instead, he focused on the path ahead, on the way the symbols seemed to pulse in time with his heartbeat. The map had brought them this far, and for better or worse, it would lead them to whatever Varunel had in store.

The shadows deepened as they walked, the air growing colder still. The city's presence loomed larger than ever, oppressive and unrelenting. And though neither of them spoke, they both felt it: Varunel wasn't done with them yet.

The mist thickened again, swirling in lazy spirals as the path narrowed. The air seemed heavier here, charged with an energy that made Kael's skin crawl. Lira walked a few paces ahead, her posture as rigid and controlled as ever, but her pace had slowed slightly. She scanned the shifting fog with a sharp gaze, her hand never straying far from the hilt of her blade.

Kael, trailing behind her, let his eyes wander to the ruins surrounding them. The crumbling arches and jagged walls seemed to lean closer, the faint glow of the map in his hand casting long, flickering shadows. He was about to call out to Lira when the mist ahead of her shifted, curling inward and forming a vague shape.

"Lira," he said cautiously, quickening his pace to catch up. "Do you see that?"

She stopped, her body tensing. "I see it."

The mist coalesced further, sharpening into the outline of a figure. It was tall and lean, draped in a flowing cloak that fluttered as if caught in a breeze that didn't exist. The face was obscured at first, but as the apparition solidified, features began to emerge—features that made Lira's breath hitch.

Kael noticed immediately. "You recognize them, don't you?"

"No," Lira said quickly, her voice hard. "It's just another trick."

"Lira," Kael said, stepping closer, his tone softer now. "You froze."

"I didn't freeze," she snapped, but the tension in her voice betrayed her. Her hand hovered over her blade as she took a step back, her eyes locked on the figure.

The apparition moved, its head tilting slightly as if studying her. Though its features were faint and blurred, there was something unnervingly familiar about its stance, its presence. Lira's grip tightened on her weapon, but she didn't draw it.

"Who is it?" Kael pressed, his voice quiet but insistent. "You know them. I can see it."

"I don't know them," Lira said through gritted teeth, her gaze never leaving the figure. "It's just this damned city playing games."

The figure raised a hand, reaching toward her, and Lira flinched—an almost imperceptible movement, but one Kael didn't miss.

"You do know them," he said, stepping into her line of sight. "Who is it, Lira? What does this place want you to see?"

"It doesn't matter," she said sharply, finally tearing her eyes away from the apparition. "None of it is real."

Kael stared at her, frustration flickering across his face. "You don't get to decide what's real and what's not. If this city is showing you something, there's a reason."

"Yeah," Lira said bitterly, "to get in my head. To make me hesitate."

"Maybe," Kael conceded. "But maybe it's showing you something you need to face."

Lira's gaze snapped to him, her eyes narrowing. "I don't need to face anything. I need to keep us alive."

Kael shook his head, his voice rising slightly. "And how do you plan to do that when you're carrying around whatever this is? Whoever this is? You can't keep pretending you're fine, Lira. This place is breaking you."

"I'm not broken," she said fiercely, her voice low and cutting. "And I don't need your armchair analysis to tell me how to deal with this city."

Kael took a step closer, lowering his voice but keeping it firm. "Then tell me who they are. If it doesn't matter, if it's not real, then tell me."

Lira's jaw tightened, and for a moment, Kael thought she might snap at him again. But then her gaze flicked back to the apparition, and something in her expression softened—just slightly. "It's no one," she said quietly. "Just someone I used to know."

Kael frowned, his tone gentler now. "Someone you lost?"

She didn't answer, her eyes fixed on the figure as it began to fade back into the mist. The silence stretched between them, heavy with the weight of things unsaid. Finally, she turned away, her voice cold again. "It doesn't matter. Let's go."

Kael hesitated, watching her retreating back. "It does matter," he said softly, though he didn't press her further. He fell into step behind her, his thoughts churning. Whatever the apparition had been, it had shaken her—and not just because of the city's influence.

For the first time, he saw cracks in the armor she wore so tightly. And though she hid it well, the vulnerability was there, buried beneath layers of deflection and denial.

As the mist closed in around them again, Kael glanced back at the spot where the figure had stood. The ruins loomed larger now, their shadows darker, their presence heavier. Varunel wasn't just testing them—it was peeling back their layers, one by one. And whether Lira admitted it or not, it had found something buried deep within her, something it wasn't going to let her ignore.

The path ahead narrowed, framed by crumbling walls and jagged stones that seemed to grow sharper with every step. The mist had thickened again, swirling around them in oppressive waves, but the faint glow of the talisman at Lira's neck provided just enough light to keep the shadows at bay.

Kael walked beside her, his face etched with tension. He kept glancing at Lira, his concern growing with every step. She hadn't spoken since the apparition—hadn't even looked at him. Her silence was heavier than the mist, pressing down on him like a weight he couldn't shake.

"Lira," he said finally, breaking the quiet. "We need to talk."

"Not now," she replied curtly, her gaze fixed on the path ahead.

"Yes, now," Kael insisted, stepping in front of her to block her path. "This isn't working."

She stopped abruptly, her hand drifting to the hilt of her blade. "What's not working?"

"This," he said, gesturing between them. "You shutting me out. Me trying to figure out what's going on with you while you act like I don't exist. We can't keep going like this."

Lira's jaw tightened, but she didn't respond immediately. She glanced past him, scanning the ruins for any sign of movement, as if hoping for an excuse to avoid the conversation.

Kael didn't let her. "I know you don't want to hear it, but we need each other to get through this. And right now, you're acting like you don't care if I'm here or not."

"I care if you're alive," she said sharply. "That's why I'm keeping us moving."

"Keeping us moving isn't enough," Kael said, his voice softening. "Not here. Not in this place. If we don't trust each other, we're not going to make it."

Lira stared at him, her eyes narrowing. "You think I don't trust you?"

"I think you don't let yourself trust anyone," Kael replied. "Not fully. You're so used to carrying everything on your own that you don't know how to let someone help you."

Her grip on her blade tightened, her knuckles white. "I don't need help."

"Yes, you do," Kael said, his tone firm but not unkind. "And so do I. This city is tearing us apart, Lira. If we keep fighting it alone, it's going to win."

Lira exhaled sharply, her gaze dropping to the ground. For a moment, the cracks in her armor were visible again—just faintly, but enough for Kael to see them.

"I've done fine on my own," she said quietly, her voice barely above a whisper.

Kael stepped closer, his tone softening further. "Maybe you have. But you're not on your own anymore. And neither am I."

She looked up at him, her expression unreadable. The silence between them stretched, filled with unspoken words and the weight of everything they'd been through. Finally, she nodded, her voice steady but quiet. "You're right. We can't do this alone."

Kael let out a breath he hadn't realized he was holding. "Then let's stop acting like we have to. From now on, we trust each other. No more shutting each other out. Agreed?"

She hesitated, her gaze flicking to the mist around them before settling back on him. "Agreed," she said, her voice firmer now. "But if you start slowing us down—"

"I won't," Kael interrupted, a faint smile tugging at the corner of his mouth. "And if you start trying to take everything on yourself, I'll remind you that you don't have to."

Lira rolled her eyes, but there was a faint glimmer of something in her expression—something that might have been gratitude. "Fine. But don't expect me to start pouring my heart out."

"Wouldn't dream of it," Kael said, his tone lighter now.

They stood there for a moment, the tension between them easing slightly. The whispers in the distance seemed quieter now, as if the city were waiting, biding its time. The path ahead was still shrouded in mist, but it didn't feel as suffocating as before.

Lira adjusted the talisman at her neck, its glow steadying her nerves. "Let's keep moving. We're not out of this yet."

Kael nodded, falling into step beside her. The air between them felt different now—not free of tension, but lighter, as if the weight of their unspoken conflict had shifted just enough to give them room to breathe.

As they moved deeper into Varunel's heart, the city seemed to shift around them, its oppressive presence still looming but less immediate. They didn't speak again, but the silence wasn't as heavy as before. For the first time, Kael felt a flicker of hope—not just for their survival, but for their partnership.

And though Lira didn't show it, the same hope stirred faintly within her, a quiet realization that she didn't have to face the city—or her fears—alone.

Chapter 7
The Shadow Within

The mist thickened as Lira and Kael moved deeper into Varunel, the city's presence bearing down on them with an almost physical weight. The whispers that had followed them through the ruined streets now shifted, morphing into faint cries and distant warnings that seemed to echo from every direction. The oppressive air seemed to sap their strength, making every step feel like a struggle.

Kael wiped sweat from his brow, his hand trembling slightly as he leaned against a fractured stone pillar. "Lira," he called out, his voice strained. "We need to stop. Just for a minute."

"We can't," Lira said curtly, her eyes scanning the shifting mist ahead. Her voice was steady, but her knuckles were white around the hilt of her blade.

Kael let out a breathless laugh, shaking his head. "You say that like we're running out of time. But time doesn't even feel real here."

She glanced back at him, her expression hard. "Stopping doesn't help us. It just gives this place more time to get inside our heads."

Kael pushed off the pillar, his frustration bubbling to the surface. "It's already in our heads, Lira. It's been in our heads since we got here. You're acting like we can just power through it, but look at us. We're exhausted."

"I'm fine," she said sharply, though her voice lacked its usual conviction.

Kael stepped closer, his tone softening despite his frustration. "No, you're not. You're trying to pretend you are, but I can see it. You're shaking."

She stiffened, her grip on her blade tightening. "I'm not shaking."

"You are," he said quietly, his eyes searching hers. "And it's okay, Lira. You don't have to hold it all together by yourself."

Lira looked away, her jaw tightening. "I don't have a choice. If I fall apart, we both die."

"That's not true," Kael said firmly. "We've made it this far because we've been working together. You don't have to do this alone."

The mist around them swirled suddenly, the whispers growing louder. The faint cries turned into something more distinct—words, half-formed but insistent.

"Turn… back…"

Kael froze, his hand instinctively moving to his weapon. "Did you hear that?"

"Of course I heard it," Lira muttered, her eyes narrowing as she scanned the shadows. "It's just the city trying to scare us."

"Well, it's working," Kael admitted, his voice trembling slightly. "Because that definitely sounded like a warning."

Lira turned to him, her expression fierce despite the exhaustion etched into her features. "And what are we supposed to do? Listen to it? Run back the way we came and hope this place lets us go?"

Kael hesitated, his gaze dropping. "I don't know. But I know we can't keep pretending this is something we can just… outlast. It's more than that, Lira. It's in us."

She exhaled slowly, her shoulders slumping slightly as the weight of his words settled over her. For a moment, the mask of stoicism she wore cracked, revealing the fear and uncertainty she'd been fighting to suppress. "I know," she said quietly. "I can feel it too."

Kael blinked, surprised by her admission. "Then why—"

"Because I can't afford to stop," she interrupted, her voice trembling slightly. "If I let it in—if I let myself feel everything this place is throwing at me—I won't be able to keep going."

Kael's frustration faded, replaced by something gentler. "You're stronger than you think, Lira. But strength doesn't mean shutting everything out. It means trusting someone to help you carry it."

She met his gaze, her eyes searching his for a long moment. The vulnerability there was raw, unguarded, and it made her feel both exposed and strangely comforted. "And what happens if you can't carry it?" she asked quietly.

"Then we fall together," Kael said simply. "But we get back up together too."

The whispers surged again, louder now, almost a scream. The air seemed to vibrate around them, the tension in the atmosphere almost unbearable. Lira gritted her teeth, her hand reaching instinctively for the talisman at her neck. The cold metal grounded her, giving her the focus she desperately needed.

"Alright," she said finally, her voice steadying. "We keep going. But if I falter—"

"You won't," Kael interrupted, his tone confident. "And if you do, I'll catch you."

She didn't respond, but the faintest hint of a smile tugged at the corner of her mouth. It was fleeting, gone almost as soon as it appeared, but it was enough.

"Come on," she said, turning back toward the path ahead. "We're close."

Kael followed, his steps lighter despite the crushing weight of the city's presence. The cries faded as they moved, replaced by a low, ominous hum that seemed to emanate from the heart of Varunel itself. The city wasn't done with them yet, but for the first time, they faced it not as two individuals, but as a team.

The air inside the cavern shifted as Kael adjusted his lantern, the faint flicker casting jagged shadows on the damp stone walls. The silence was thick, interrupted only by the occasional drip of water from unseen crevices. Kael noticed Lira walking ahead, her shoulders stiff and her grip on her blade unnaturally tight. Her usually fluid movements had become clipped, mechanical.

"You're tense," Kael said, his voice cutting through the quiet.

"I'm focused," Lira shot back, not slowing her pace.

Kael quickened his steps to match hers. "No, this is different. Varunel is getting to you, isn't it?"

She paused for a fraction of a second before resuming her march. "I'm fine, Kael. Drop it."

But Kael didn't. He reached out, placing a firm hand on her arm to stop her. "Lira, it's okay to feel it. This place—it's not just dangerous; it's oppressive. Pretending it doesn't affect you won't help either of us."

She turned to face him, her expression a careful mask of indifference, though her eyes betrayed a flicker of unease. "And what would you know about it?"

Kael sighed, his hand dropping back to his side. "More than I'd like." He stepped back, leaning against the cold stone wall, and ran a hand through his dark, sweat-dampened hair. "You know, on my first real mission, I was convinced I'd never feel fear. I'd trained for years, told myself I was ready for anything. Then we were sent to the Scarred Pass."

Lira frowned. "The Scarred Pass? That place is—"

"A death trap," Kael finished for her. "Yeah. It was supposed to be a simple retrieval. But everything about that place felt wrong, just like Varunel. The air was heavy, the shadows moved when they shouldn't have, and no amount of logic or training could shake the feeling that something was watching us."

Lira tilted her head slightly, her grip on the blade relaxing. "What happened?"

Kael's jaw tightened, and for a moment, he seemed to retreat into the memory. "We got what we came for. But we lost two of our team. Not because we were outnumbered or outmatched—but because fear made us reckless. I almost didn't make it out myself." He looked directly at her now, his voice steady but laced with an unmistakable vulnerability. "I've learned since then that admitting I'm afraid doesn't make me weak. It makes me cautious. And that's what keeps me alive."

Lira crossed her arms, her gaze dropping to the uneven floor. "It's not fear," she said after a pause, her voice softer than before.

"Then what is it?" Kael asked gently.

"It's..." She hesitated, struggling for words. "It's the way this place feels. Like it's trying to unravel me. Every step deeper feels like I'm losing a piece of myself."

Kael nodded slowly. "That's what this place does. Varunel gets into your head, twists your thoughts. But we're here together, Lira. You don't have to face this alone."

She glanced at him, her expression unreadable for a moment before a small, almost imperceptible nod. "Maybe... maybe I don't. But don't expect me to start sharing my deepest fears."

Kael chuckled, the sound lightening the oppressive mood slightly. "Fair enough. Baby steps, right?"

"Don't push your luck," she muttered, though there was a faint smile tugging at her lips.

As they resumed their journey, the tension between them eased, if only slightly. Kael noticed the subtle shift in Lira's posture—still alert, but no longer rigid with denial. The unspoken bond of trust between them had grown, a fragile thread that might just be strong enough to see them through the unknown depths of Varunel.

The tunnel widened into an unexpected chamber, its expanse lost in the gloom. The walls glimmered faintly, etched with lines of pale light that pulsed like a heartbeat. Kael stopped in his tracks, his sharp intake of breath echoing faintly. Lira's fingers clenched around the talisman hanging from her neck, the metal warm against her palm.

"This isn't on the map," Kael muttered, his voice low as his eyes scanned the surroundings.

Lira took a step forward, her boots crunching against a brittle layer of crystalline dust. "No, it isn't," she said, her voice tight. The whispers were louder here, a susurration that gnawed at the edges of her thoughts. Words she couldn't quite decipher pressed against her mind like waves against a weakening dam.

Kael squinted, tilting his lantern toward the faintly glowing walls. The light from the flame seemed to ripple, distorting unnaturally. "This place… it feels alive," he said.

"Alive and watching," Lira added, her voice barely above a whisper.

A shadow darted across the edge of her vision. Lira spun, raising her blade, but there was nothing. The shadows themselves seemed to writhe, folding and unfolding like smoke caught in an invisible wind.

Kael moved to her side, his tone urgent. "Lira, the talisman. It's reacting."

She looked down. The talisman's faint glow was now a steady pulse, matching the rhythm of the walls. Its warmth was almost unbearable, as though it were warning her of something unseen.

"We need to stop," Kael said firmly.

Lira shot him a wary glance. "Stop? Here? You're joking."

"No," he said, stepping closer to meet her gaze. "We need to use the talisman. Whatever this place is, it's amplifying Varunel's power. Look at it."

She hesitated, her grip tightening around the artifact. "I know what it's doing. But activating it could draw more attention to us."

"And doing nothing might let this place tear us apart from the inside," Kael countered, his voice rising slightly. "You're fighting it already, aren't you? The whispers, the shadows—they're in your head too."

Lira's jaw clenched. She didn't want to admit it, but he was right. The longer they stayed here, the harder it became to separate her thoughts from the insidious whispers.

"You think the talisman will shield us?" she asked, her tone skeptical but laced with the barest hint of hope.

Kael nodded. "It has to. This thing was made to counteract Varunel's influence. If it works, we can clear our minds, regroup, and figure out what this place is without losing ourselves."

Lira looked down at the talisman again, its glow now almost mesmerizing. Her fingers trembled, betraying the internal battle raging within her. "And if it doesn't work?"

"Then we keep moving," Kael said, his voice resolute. "But standing here debating won't help. Trust me on this, Lira."

For a moment, she said nothing. The chamber seemed to close in around them, the whispers swelling, growing louder. Her breath quickened, and she could feel her grip on reality slipping.

Finally, she nodded. "Fine. But don't expect me to trust this thing completely."

"Good enough for me," Kael said, stepping back to give her space.

Lira closed her eyes and held the talisman out before her, focusing on its warmth. The glow brightened, spreading outward in faint waves that pushed back the oppressive atmosphere. The whispers receded, their intensity dulled.

Kael let out a slow breath. "It's working."

Lira opened her eyes, relief flickering across her face before she schooled her expression back to neutrality. "For now," she said, her voice steadier.

The room seemed less alive, the pulsing walls dimming slightly. But the shadows still lingered, moving at the edges of their vision.

Kael reached out, gripping her shoulder briefly. "We'll get through this, Lira. One step at a time."

She nodded, her gaze sweeping the chamber once more. "Let's hope this thing keeps working. Because whatever this place is, it's not done with us yet."

With renewed determination, they pressed forward, the talisman's glow their only shield against the encroaching darkness.

The oppressive air pressed down on them like an invisible weight, but they found a small, flat ledge where they could rest. Kael slumped against the wall, his lantern casting flickering shadows over the jagged rocks. Lira sat a few feet away, her knees drawn up and the talisman still clutched in her hand.

For a while, neither of them spoke. The silence was thick, broken only by the distant drip of water and the occasional scrape of boots on stone.

Kael glanced at her, his voice soft but tinged with curiosity. "You're quieter than usual. That's how I know something's eating at you."

Lira exhaled sharply, not quite a laugh but not entirely dismissive either. "I didn't think my silence would stand out here. This whole place feels like it's swallowing every sound."

"It does," Kael agreed, shifting to face her more directly. "But it's not just the place. It's you. You've been carrying something since the start of this mission—since before we even got here. I can see it."

Lira didn't respond immediately. She stared at the talisman, its glow subdued but steady. Her voice, when it came, was low, almost a whisper. "Why are you always trying to get me to talk, Kael? What makes you think I want to?"

Kael leaned forward, resting his arms on his knees. "Because I've been where you are. Trying to shoulder everything alone, telling myself I didn't need anyone. It doesn't work, Lira. And it's not who you are, no matter how much you try to pretend."

Her fingers tightened around the talisman, her knuckles white. For a moment, Kael thought she'd shut him out again. Then, to his surprise, she spoke.

"I've failed before," she said, her voice barely audible.

Kael frowned. "Failed? At what?"

Lira's gaze didn't lift from the talisman. "A mission. Years ago. I made a mistake, a stupid one. People relied on me, and I let them down. They paid the price for my arrogance."

"Lira..."

"Don't," she said sharply, her eyes snapping to his. The raw emotion in her voice silenced him. "You wanted me to talk, so listen. After that, I promised myself I'd never let anyone else pay for my weakness. I'd get stronger. Smarter. I wouldn't need anyone else to carry me."

Kael sat back, his expression softening. "And that's why you're here. Because you think you have to do this alone."

Lira hesitated, then nodded. "Varunel isn't just a mission for me. It's a chance to prove that I can face my past. That I'm not the same person who made that mistake."

Kael let the silence stretch for a moment before he spoke. "You know, strength isn't about doing everything alone. Sometimes it's about knowing when to trust someone else to stand with you."

She scoffed, but the sound lacked its usual edge. "That sounds like something out of a training manual."

Kael grinned faintly. "Maybe. Doesn't mean it's not true. Look, you've been through hell—that's clear. But you're not the only one fighting. I'm here too, and I'm not going to let you carry this alone, no matter how stubborn you are."

Lira's lips twitched, almost forming a smile. "You really don't know when to back off, do you?"

"Not when it comes to keeping my allies alive," Kael said, his tone light but firm.

She looked away, her grip on the talisman loosening slightly. "I don't know if I can change, Kael. I've spent so long telling myself I had to be unbreakable. Letting that go... it's terrifying."

Kael's voice softened further. "No one's unbreakable, Lira. Not you, not me. But we're stronger together. And if Varunel thinks it can break us, it's got another thing coming."

For the first time, Lira let out a genuine laugh—short and quiet, but real. She glanced at him, the faintest trace of gratitude in her eyes. "You're insufferable, you know that?"

Kael leaned back with a smirk. "I've been called worse."

Lira shook her head, the moment of levity easing the tension in her posture. She didn't say it outright, but Kael could sense the shift. The walls Lira had built around herself were beginning to crack, and in their place, a tentative trust was starting to grow.

As they stood to continue their journey, the oppressive weight of Varunel felt just a little lighter. For the first time, they weren't just two individuals fighting their own battles—they were allies, moving forward together.

Chapter 8
The Fragmented Path

The cavernous hallway opened into a vast chamber that hummed with latent energy. The air was thicker here, charged with an unsettling mix of dread and anticipation. Shadows that had once lingered at the edges of their vision now morphed into tangible figures, flickering in and out of existence like an old, fading projection.

Kael slowed his pace, his eyes narrowing as he tried to make sense of the shifting forms. "Do you see that?"

Lira, a few steps ahead, paused and turned. Her gaze followed his, locking onto a particular shadow. It had taken the shape of a woman, her form delicate but obscured by an ethereal haze. As they watched, the figure solidified, her features becoming clearer with each passing second.

"She's crying," Kael said, his voice low and cautious.

The woman's face was etched with anguish, her hands clawing at the air as though she were reaching for something—or someone—just beyond her grasp. Her voice, though faint and fragmented, carried an undeniable plea.

"Help me... please... I can't escape..."

Kael took an involuntary step forward. "She's calling out. We can't just ignore that."

"Stop," Lira said sharply, grabbing his arm. Her grip was firm, her tone unyielding. "You don't know what this is. It could be a trick."

He pulled his arm free, though he didn't move closer to the apparition. "You think everything is a trap, Lira. Look at her—she's terrified."

"And what if that's exactly what Varunel wants us to see?" she countered, her voice cutting through the tense air. "This city has been playing with our heads since we got here. You've felt it, Kael. The whispers, the shadows—it's not just background noise. It's deliberate."

Kael hesitated, his eyes flicking between Lira and the crying woman. The figure seemed so real, so human. Her sobs grew louder, more insistent, and Kael felt a pang of guilt gnawing at him.

"Lira, what if it's not a trick? What if she's trapped here, just like us? What if we can help her?"

Lira's jaw tightened, but she didn't look away from the figure. Her hand drifted to the talisman around her neck, the artifact vibrating faintly against her skin. "And what if responding to her is exactly how we end up like her? Look at her, Kael. She's desperate, yes—but does she look alive to you?"

Kael stared at the woman again. Her form flickered, and for a brief moment, her face twisted into something unrecognizable—a visage of despair so profound it felt inhuman. Then, just as quickly, it shifted back to her pleading, tear-streaked expression.

He swallowed hard. "I don't know, Lira. But I can't just stand here and do nothing."

"You're not thinking straight," she said, stepping closer to block his path. "That's what this place does. It preys on your instincts, your empathy. But if you give in, you're handing Varunel the key to your mind."

Kael's shoulders sagged, frustration and uncertainty warring within him. "And what if you're wrong? What if this is the one time someone really does need us, and we turn our backs?"

Lira softened slightly, her tone shifting from harsh to firm but understanding. "If this city had good intentions, it wouldn't be hiding behind illusions and whispers. I get it—you want to help. But here, caution is survival. You said it yourself back in the Scarred Pass: being reckless costs lives."

Kael closed his eyes, taking a slow breath to steady himself. "You're right. I hate it, but you're right."

The woman's sobs continued, each one tugging at Kael's resolve, but he forced himself to take a step back. Lira nodded, her expression a mixture of relief and lingering tension.

"Let's keep moving," she said, her voice softer now. "Whatever this is, it's not our fight. Not yet."

As they turned to leave, the figure's cries intensified, her outstretched hands reaching for them as though begging them to stay. Kael clenched his fists, his jaw tightening as he fought the urge to turn back.

The woman's voice echoed behind them as they walked away, fading into a chilling silence.

"You did the right thing," Lira said quietly, though she didn't sound entirely convinced herself.

Kael didn't respond, his mind still grappling with the image of the woman's desperate face. As the shadows around them shifted once more, he couldn't shake the feeling that Varunel wasn't just showing them its memories—it was testing them. And the worst was yet to come.

The passage narrowed as they continued, the air growing heavier with each step. The flickering shadows from their lanterns seemed more restless here, as if Varunel's past was closer to the surface. Lira's gaze darted from one shifting form to another, her usual wariness tinged with something else—curiosity.

Kael walked a few paces behind her, his sharp eyes scanning the surroundings. "You're quieter than usual again," he said, his tone casual but probing.

Lira didn't respond right away. She slowed her pace, her attention fixed on an apparition forming ahead. It was faint at first, a shapeless blur of light and shadow, but as they approached, it coalesced into the image of a young boy. He sat on the ground, his arms wrapped tightly around his knees, rocking back and forth.

Kael stepped closer, peering over her shoulder. "Another one," he said softly.

"He's not like the others," Lira murmured. Her voice was low, almost reverent, as though speaking too loudly might shatter the fragile scene before them.

Kael frowned. "How do you mean?"

"He's not crying or pleading. He's just... there. Quiet. Resigned."

The boy's form flickered, his movements slowing as if he sensed their presence. Lira found herself inching closer, her skepticism momentarily eclipsed by something she couldn't quite name.

Kael noticed her change in demeanor and tilted his head. "You're staring at him like you want to reach out."

"Maybe I do," Lira admitted, surprising herself with her honesty. She straightened, her usual guardedness returning as she added, "Don't read too much into it."

Kael raised an eyebrow but chose not to press. Instead, he gestured toward the boy. "You think he's real? Or is this just another of Varunel's tricks?"

Lira hesitated, her fingers brushing the talisman around her neck. "I don't know. But it doesn't feel like the others. It's less... malevolent."

"That doesn't mean it's safe," Kael pointed out, his voice cautious.

She nodded slowly but didn't move away. "It's not just that. It's like..." She trailed off, searching for the right words. "Like we're seeing pieces of something. Fragments. Memories, maybe. But memories of what? People's souls? Their pain? Or is this just the curse itself, echoing through the city?"

Kael crossed his arms, watching her carefully. "I thought you were the one telling me not to trust anything here. Now you're the one getting drawn in."

Lira turned to him, her expression unreadable. "I'm not trusting it. I'm trying to understand it. There's a difference."

"Is there?" Kael asked, his tone laced with a hint of humor. "Because from where I'm standing, it looks like you're starting to empathize with ghosts."

She huffed, but there was no venom in it. "Maybe I am. Or maybe I'm just tired of fighting everything. Have you ever stopped to think that understanding this place might be the key to surviving it?"

Kael studied her for a moment, his usual quick retorts replaced by thoughtful silence. "Fair point," he said at last. "But understanding something doesn't mean letting your guard down. That's a fine line, Lira."

"I know that," she snapped, though her voice lacked its usual sharpness. "I'm not letting my guard down. I just... I can't stop thinking about what these visions are. If they're memories, then who left them behind? And why?"

Kael softened slightly, hearing the genuine curiosity—and perhaps a trace of vulnerability—in her voice. "It's progress, you know," he said after a moment.

Lira frowned. "What is?"

"You," he said simply. "You're actually considering something beyond just surviving this mission. You're asking questions. Letting yourself feel something about this place, even if you don't trust it."

She scoffed, but a faint smirk tugged at her lips. "Don't start thinking you're some kind of mentor, Kael. I'm just trying to figure out how to get through this without losing my mind."

"Sure," Kael said, a grin playing at the edges of his mouth. "Keep telling yourself that."

Lira rolled her eyes and turned her attention back to the boy. His form was fading now, the edges of his image dissolving into mist. For a moment, she felt a pang of regret, as though she'd lost the chance to understand something important.

"Let's keep moving," she said abruptly, her tone more resolute.

Kael nodded, falling into step beside her. As they walked, he couldn't help but notice the subtle shift in her demeanor. She wasn't just surviving anymore—she was engaging with the world around her, even if it was a cursed and broken one.

And for the first time, Kael felt a flicker of hope that Varunel might not break them after all.

The air grew colder as the corridor widened into another chamber, its walls shimmering with faint, iridescent light. The flickering forms of past memories danced like fireflies, more vivid now than before. Lira moved cautiously, her fingers brushing the hilt of her blade, her every sense on high alert.

Kael walked a step behind her, his own focus split between scanning the area and watching Lira. She had been quieter since their last stop, her usual sharpness dulled into something Kael could only describe as haunted.

The shadows ahead coalesced, forming a scene that froze Lira in her tracks. The outline of a figure appeared—a man, tall and broad-shouldered, with hair that caught the faint light like a halo. He stood with his back to them, his posture tense, as though bracing for something unseen.

Kael squinted, stepping closer to Lira. "Do you recognize him?"

Lira didn't answer. Her grip on her blade tightened, her knuckles turning white.

The memory grew clearer. The man turned slightly, his profile catching the light. His expression was one of grim determination, his eyes scanning the shadows as if expecting an attack. Around him, the faint forms of other figures began to take shape, their movements panicked and chaotic.

Kael's gaze darted to Lira. "Lira?" he asked softly.

Her jaw was clenched, her eyes fixed on the scene before her. She didn't move, her body rigid as though rooted to the spot.

"Lira, talk to me," Kael said, his tone more insistent.

"It's nothing," she said quickly, her voice clipped. "Just another vision. Let's keep moving."

Kael frowned, stepping in front of her. "It's not nothing. You know him, don't you?"

"I said it's nothing," she snapped, her voice sharper now. She pushed past him, her steps quick and deliberate as if she could outrun the memory.

But the vision followed them. The figures moved in tandem with Lira's pace, their forms shifting but always staying just ahead. The man's face came into full view now, and Kael could see the resemblance to someone in Lira's past—someone important.

"You can't just ignore this," Kael said, hurrying to catch up with her.

"Watch me," she muttered, not breaking stride.

The memory intensified. The man's voice echoed through the chamber, faint but distinct enough to send a chill down Kael's spine.

"Get out of here! Now!" the man yelled, his voice filled with urgency and fear.

Lira froze again, her breathing uneven. The scene replayed, the man's words looping like a broken record. The chaos around him grew, the shadowy figures collapsing into indistinct shapes as the man stood firm, his body shielding something unseen.

Kael stepped closer, his voice gentle but firm. "Lira, this isn't just a random memory. This is about you, isn't it?"

Her shoulders stiffened, and for a moment, Kael thought she wouldn't respond. Then she turned to him, her eyes flashing with barely contained emotion.

"It doesn't matter," she said through gritted teeth. "It's in the past."

"Clearly, it does matter," Kael said, refusing to back down. "This place is digging into you. You can't just shove it aside."

Lira shook her head, her expression a mix of anger and pain. "What do you want me to say, Kael? That I lost someone? That I wasn't strong enough to save him? That this—" she gestured to the vision, her voice cracking slightly, "—is exactly how it happened? Because it is. And I can't change that."

Kael stepped closer, his tone softening. "I'm not asking you to change it, Lira. I'm asking you to let yourself feel it. You're not going to win this fight by pretending it doesn't hurt."

Her gaze dropped, her fists clenched at her sides. The memory continued to play out, the man's figure growing fainter with each loop.

"I can't," she whispered, her voice barely audible.

"You can," Kael said gently. "You're not the same person you were then. And you're not alone this time."

Lira closed her eyes, her breathing shallow as she fought against the weight of her emotions. The man's figure faded completely now, leaving only the echo of his voice behind.

When she opened her eyes again, they were glassy but resolute. "We need to keep moving," she said, her voice steadier but still fragile.

Kael nodded, not pushing her further. As they resumed their path, he stayed close, his presence a silent reassurance.

Though the vision had disappeared, its impact lingered, casting a heavy shadow over their journey. Lira's walls were still up, but Kael could see the cracks beginning to form, the vulnerability she had fought so hard to suppress now impossible to ignore.

The corridor narrowed into a jagged path, the air colder now, biting at their skin. The shadows around them grew sharper, their movements deliberate rather than random. Kael kept close to Lira, his lantern held high, casting flickering light on the uneven walls.

"Lira, we need to stop for a second," Kael said, his tone steady but concerned.

"I'm fine," Lira replied tersely, her voice tight.

Kael wasn't convinced, but he didn't press her. They had barely gone another dozen steps when the air around them shifted. A shadow peeled itself away from the wall ahead, forming into a figure that was unnervingly real. It was a man—not the same one from before—but his posture and expression bore the weight of familiarity.

"Lira," the figure said, its voice resonating through the chamber.

Both of them froze.

Kael glanced at her, his hand moving instinctively to his weapon. "Did that thing just say your name?"

"It's a trick," Lira muttered, though her voice wavered. She tightened her grip on the talisman around her neck, its faint glow flickering as if in protest.

The figure stepped closer, its features more distinct now. The man looked directly at Lira, his expression solemn. "You've always been stubborn. That's what got me killed."

Kael's eyes widened. "Lira, what is this? Who is he?"

"It's not real," she said through clenched teeth, though she didn't move. Her eyes were locked on the apparition, a mix of defiance and fear in her gaze.

The figure tilted its head, its voice softening. "You couldn't let go, even when you knew the odds. You think you're stronger now, but you're just hiding behind walls. How long before you fail again?"

Kael stepped forward, placing himself slightly in front of Lira. "Alright, that's enough. Whatever you are, you're not going to get in her head."

The figure ignored him, its gaze fixed on Lira. "You can't run from this, Lira. Varunel doesn't forget. Neither should you."

"Shut up," she hissed, her hand trembling as she raised her blade.

Kael reached out, his voice firm but calm. "Lira, don't. That's what it wants—to push you over the edge. You can't give it that power."

The apparition faded slightly, its edges dissolving into mist. But its voice lingered, echoing in the chamber. "You'll break eventually. They always do."

Lira's blade dropped slightly, her breathing uneven. She turned away, her free hand gripping the talisman so tightly her knuckles were white.

Kael placed a hand on her shoulder, his voice soft. "Hey. Don't let it get to you. That thing—it's not him. Whatever it's saying, it's just trying to mess with your head."

She shook him off, her voice sharp but brittle. "You think I don't know that? You think I don't see what this place is doing to me?"

"Then talk to me," Kael said, stepping in front of her. "Stop bottling it up like you have to carry it all yourself. That's what Varunel wants—your silence, your fear. Don't let it win."

Lira hesitated, her gaze fixed on the ground. The talisman in her hand pulsed faintly, its warmth grounding her even as her thoughts spiraled.

"I've spent years trying to bury that day," she admitted finally, her voice barely above a whisper. "And now it's here, in my face, ripping open everything I tried to forget."

Kael nodded slowly. "And that's what this place does. It finds your cracks and pries them open. But, Lira, that doesn't mean you have to fight it alone."

Her eyes lifted to meet his, a flicker of vulnerability showing through her usual guarded expression. "What if I can't? What if this is too much?"

Kael's voice was steady, his gaze unwavering. "You can, because you're not doing it alone. I'm here. And we're getting through this together, one step at a time."

Lira exhaled shakily, some of the tension leaving her shoulders. She glanced at the shadows around them, now quieter but still oppressive.

"Together, then," she said, her voice steadier.

Kael grinned faintly, stepping back to let her take the lead again. "Good. Because there's no way I'm letting you leave me to face this mess solo."

The two of them pressed forward, their steps more deliberate now. The shadows seemed to retreat slightly, though the weight of Varunel's influence still hung heavy around them. But for the first time, Lira didn't feel completely alone in the fight.

The path ahead was still uncertain, but with Kael by her side, she felt a flicker of resolve she hadn't allowed herself to feel in years. Together, they would face whatever Varunel had in store.

Chapter 9
A Fateful Encounter

The tunnel felt tighter, the oppressive darkness closing in around them like a living thing. Lira held the map in front of her, its once-glowing symbols now dim and flickering. The lines shifted erratically, rearranging themselves in a pattern that refused to stay still.

"Damn it," she muttered, shaking the map as if that would force it to cooperate.

Kael glanced over her shoulder, his brow furrowing. "That's not exactly reassuring. How are we supposed to navigate if the map doesn't even know where we are?"

Lira shot him a glare, her frustration barely contained. "It worked before. Maybe it just needs—" She stopped, watching as the symbols blinked out entirely, leaving the parchment blank. Her voice dropped, a mix of disbelief and anger. "What is this?"

Kael leaned closer, his expression skeptical. "Maybe it's reacting to the city. Varunel's messing with everything else—why not the map?"

She crumpled the map in her fist, her jaw tightening. "This isn't just 'messing with us.' This was supposed to guide us through, Kael. Elder Thorne said it would be reliable."

Kael raised an eyebrow. "And you believed him? The guy who handed us cursed artifacts to walk into a haunted city? Seems like maybe we should've taken his advice with a grain of salt."

Lira turned away, gripping the talisman around her neck. Its glow was faint, flickering like a dying ember. "The talisman isn't much better," she said quietly. "It's supposed to push back the whispers, but they're louder now. Clearer."

Kael tilted his head, studying her. "What are they saying?"

She hesitated, her fingers tightening around the artifact. "It's... fragments. Taunts. Telling me I'll fail, that I'll lose everything again. They're not just whispers anymore—they're inside my head."

Kael stepped closer, his voice firm but calm. "And you think the talisman's supposed to fix that?"

"It's what it was made for!" she snapped, her voice echoing in the narrow space. "It's what Thorne said would protect us, and now it's useless!"

Kael crossed his arms, his tone softening. "Maybe it's not useless. Maybe we're just leaning on it too much. Look, I get it—having something tangible to hold onto makes this easier. But maybe it's not enough."

"Not enough?" Lira spun to face him, her frustration spilling over. "Kael, this isn't about 'leaning too much.' These artifacts were the plan. The only plan. Without them, we're walking blind into a city that wants us dead."

"Then maybe we stop relying on them like they're infallible," Kael said, his voice rising slightly. "Maybe we start relying on something else—our instincts, our guts. You've been through worse, Lira. You didn't have a glowing necklace or a magic map then. You made it out because you're smart, and you don't give up. That's what's going to get us through this, not a bunch of trinkets."

Lira opened her mouth to argue but stopped, her gaze dropping to the talisman. Its flicker had grown steadier, but it was still faint, almost as if it were responding to her inner turmoil.

"And what if you're wrong?" she asked after a moment, her voice quieter.

Kael shrugged, a faint grin tugging at his lips. "Then we die horribly in a haunted city. But at least we'll know we didn't sit around waiting for a piece of glowing rock to save us."

Despite herself, Lira let out a short, bitter laugh. "That's your idea of a pep talk?"

"Hey, I'm trying here," Kael said, his grin widening. "Look, we've made it this far, right? Varunel hasn't broken us yet. And it won't, as long as we keep moving. Artifacts or no artifacts."

Lira sighed, her shoulders relaxing slightly. She uncrumpled the map and smoothed it out against her leg, though the symbols remained stubbornly absent. "Fine. But if your 'gut instinct' gets us killed, I'm haunting you for eternity."

Kael chuckled. "Deal. But don't worry—I'm betting on us making it out alive."

She shook her head, a faint smirk on her lips. "You're insufferable, you know that?"

"Yeah, but you'd miss me if I wasn't," he replied, already stepping forward to take the lead.

As they continued deeper into the twisting tunnels, the whispers grew louder, and the artifacts dimmer. But for the first time, Lira felt the faintest flicker of something she hadn't allowed herself to feel in years—trust. If the artifacts failed completely, they still had each other.

And for now, that was enough.

The corridor opened abruptly into a vast courtyard, its expanse barely illuminated by the faint glow of their lanterns. The oppressive darkness here was deeper, heavier, pressing against their senses like a living thing. The air felt alive, humming with an energy that made the hair on the back of Kael's neck stand on end.

"This is it," Lira said, holding up the map. She pointed to the faint outline of a symbol still visible on the crumpled parchment. "This is the spot the map led us to."

Kael surveyed the courtyard. The shadows shifted unnaturally, refusing to settle into place. At the edges of the light, faint shapes moved, too indistinct to identify.

"Convenient," he muttered, his voice tinged with sarcasm. "A courtyard in the middle of nowhere, surrounded by creepy shadows. Nothing ominous about this at all."

Lira ignored him, focusing instead on the map. The symbol on the parchment flickered and began to distort, as though the city itself were rewriting its purpose.

"Not again," she muttered under her breath.

Before Kael could respond, the whispers intensified. No longer faint murmurs, the voices rose in clarity, each syllable sharp and deliberate.

"Kael... Lira..."

Both of them froze.

"That's new," Kael said, his voice low.

"It's the city," Lira replied, her grip tightening on the map. "It's trying to mess with us. Don't let it."

Kael tilted his head, listening carefully. The voices weren't random. They called their names with a strange cadence, almost musical, but laced with malice.

"I don't think it's just trying to mess with us," he said. "It's guiding us."

"Guiding us?" Lira shot him a sharp look. "To what? Our deaths?"

"Maybe," Kael admitted, his tone light despite the weight of his words. "But if Varunel's calling us, it means there's something here it doesn't want us to find—or something it's daring us to see."

"That's a hell of a gamble," Lira said, folding the map and tucking it into her pack. "And you're basing this on... what? A feeling?"

Kael turned to her, his expression steady. "Yeah, a feeling. Look, the map's not helping, and the talisman's barely holding up. What if we stop fighting Varunel's signals and try following them instead?"

"Because that's exactly what it wants us to do," Lira said, her skepticism sharp.

"Or it's what it thinks we won't do because we're too scared," Kael countered. He took a step forward, his lantern casting a wider glow over the courtyard. The shadows writhed but didn't retreat.

Lira hesitated, torn between her ingrained caution and the strange logic in Kael's suggestion. "You're really willing to bet our lives on this?"

Kael glanced back at her, his grin faint but confident. "You said it yourself earlier—sometimes you've got to trust your instincts. This is me doing that. You coming?"

She sighed heavily, muttering under her breath. "You're going to get us killed."

Kael chuckled. "Probably. But not today."

Reluctantly, Lira followed as Kael moved deeper into the courtyard. The voices grew louder, their tone shifting from taunting to something almost pleading.

"This is insane," Lira said, her voice hushed.

"Maybe," Kael replied, scanning the area. His steps were deliberate, his eyes fixed on the subtle patterns in the shadows. He stopped suddenly, pointing to a faintly glowing marking on the ground. "There. That's what they're leading us to."

Lira squinted, stepping closer to examine the marking. It was an intricate sigil, etched into the stone and pulsing faintly with a rhythm that matched the city's whispers.

"What is it?" she asked.

Kael shrugged. "A clue, maybe. Or a trap. Either way, it's something."

Lira knelt beside the sigil, her skepticism giving way to curiosity. The glow from the marking seemed to respond to her presence, growing slightly brighter.

"It's connected to the whispers," she said.

"Exactly," Kael replied, kneeling beside her. "Which means we're on the right track."

"For now," Lira muttered, but there was less doubt in her voice.

As the whispers swirled around them, Lira felt the faintest glimmer of hope, a flicker of belief that Kael's instincts might be their best chance at surviving Varunel's games. For the first time, she allowed herself to follow rather than lead, trusting in the growing confidence of her companion.

Together, they studied the sigil, ready to face whatever secrets it might reveal.

The air in the courtyard shifted, growing colder and heavier. The shadows writhed as if alive, the faint whispers surrounding Kael and Lira turning into an eerie symphony of voices. Then, the environment began to change. The edges of the courtyard blurred, the walls fading into a haze as the ground beneath their feet transformed into uneven stone.

Kael looked around, his breath visible in the icy air. "This... isn't the courtyard anymore."

Lira stood frozen, her gaze locked on a new vision forming in the mist ahead. It was a house, small and modest, with flowers blooming in a well-tended garden. A man and a young girl stood on the porch, their faces etched with joy. The girl waved to someone unseen, her laughter carrying on the wind.

"Lira," Kael said, his tone cautious.

She didn't respond. Her hand gripped the talisman tightly, but its glow remained dim. "That's... impossible," she whispered.

Kael stepped closer, placing a hand on her shoulder. "What is it? Do you know them?"

Lira's jaw tightened. "It's my sister and my father. This is... it's my home. Before..." Her voice trailed off, and she took an involuntary step toward the vision.

But as she moved, the scene shifted abruptly. The flowers withered, the house crumbled, and the figures disappeared, replaced by an overwhelming emptiness. Lira stopped, her breath catching in her throat.

Kael grabbed her arm, pulling her back. "Hey, don't let it pull you in. It's not real, Lira."

"I know that!" she snapped, but her voice trembled.

Kael frowned, then turned as a new vision emerged nearby. This one was his—a battlefield, littered with the bodies of fallen comrades. He saw himself standing in the center, younger, bloodied, and clutching a sword with trembling hands.

"No," he muttered, shaking his head. "This isn't real either."

The vision of his past self turned to him, its face contorted with anger and pain. "You left us," it said, its voice cold and accusing. "You ran."

Kael's fists clenched. "I didn't run. I did what I had to do to survive."

"At their expense," the apparition spat.

Kael felt a hand on his arm. He turned to see Lira watching him, her own struggle momentarily forgotten. "Kael, listen to your own advice," she said. "It's not real. Don't let it in."

He took a deep breath, nodding. "You're right. We can't give it that power."

The visions around them flickered, shifting again, the environment morphing into a series of fragmented scenes—Kael's regrets, Lira's fears, and memories of people they had lost. The weight of the city's psychological assault pressed down on them, threatening to crack their resolve.

"This place knows how to hit where it hurts," Lira said bitterly, her voice shaking.

Kael nodded. "It's trying to break us. But we're not going to let it." He paused, then added, "We need to ground ourselves—stay present. Maybe if we keep each other talking, it won't have as much of a hold on us."

Lira raised an eyebrow. "Talking? That's your big strategy?"

"Got a better one?" Kael shot back.

She hesitated, then sighed. "Fine. What do we talk about?"

Kael thought for a moment, his gaze darting between the flickering memories. "Tell me about your sister. What was she like?"

Lira stiffened but didn't pull away. After a long pause, she said, "She was... bright. Always smiling. She used to sing while she worked in the garden. I hated how much she sang back then, but now..." Her voice faltered.

Kael offered a small smile. "Sounds like she was amazing."

"She was," Lira said, her tone softening. "What about you? What was your first mission like?"

Kael chuckled bitterly. "A disaster. We were supposed to secure a small outpost, but everything went wrong. Poor planning, bad intel—it was chaos. I was convinced I wouldn't make it out."

"But you did," Lira said, watching him closely.

"Yeah," Kael said, his voice quieter. "But not everyone did."

The tension in the air seemed to ease slightly as they continued trading memories, their voices grounding them in the present. The visions still swirled around them, but their intensity waned, as though the city's grip was loosening.

"We're not beating this place," Lira said after a while, her tone thoughtful. "But we're not letting it beat us either."

"Exactly," Kael replied, his determination clear. "We just keep moving forward. Together."

For the first time since entering Varunel, Lira felt a flicker of hope. The city's whispers might haunt them, but they weren't fighting alone—and that made all the difference.

The air rippled around them, and the darkness of the courtyard gave way to a stark, frozen tableau. A massive square stretched out before them, littered with the remnants of what might once have been a thriving part of Varunel. Buildings lay in ruin, their walls crumbled, and the ground was cracked and blackened, as though scorched by fire. In the center of it all stood a towering monument, fractured down the middle and leaning precariously.

Kael stopped, staring at the scene. "This isn't just another vision," he said, his voice heavy with realization. "This... this feels like the city itself."

Lira nodded, her grip on her blade tightening. "It's a memory," she said softly. "A moment frozen in time. Something that mattered to Varunel."

Around them, ghostly figures began to appear, moving soundlessly through the devastation. Some carried what looked like supplies, others tended to the wounded. The weight of their collective despair was palpable, pressing down on Kael and Lira like a physical force.

Kael turned to her. "Do you feel that? It's like... it's alive. Like it's mourning."

Lira didn't answer. Her gaze was locked on a figure in the distance—a woman, standing alone amidst the destruction. Her back was to them, but there was something familiar in the way she stood, her shoulders heavy with grief.

"Lira?" Kael asked, stepping closer to her.

"She's... me," Lira said, her voice barely above a whisper.

Kael's brow furrowed. "What are you talking about?"

"Not literally," Lira clarified, shaking her head. "But I know that stance. I've felt it. That moment when you're standing in the middle of everything you've lost and all you can think about is what you could've done differently."

Kael studied her, his expression softening. "You've been holding that in this whole time, haven't you?"

She let out a bitter laugh, her hands trembling slightly as she gripped the talisman around her neck. "What's the point of saying it out loud? It doesn't change anything. I failed before, and now I'm here, in this cursed city, trying not to do it again. But every step we take, I feel like I'm walking right into another failure."

"Lira," Kael said, stepping in front of her and forcing her to meet his gaze. "You haven't failed here. You're still fighting. And trust me, this city isn't going to let either of us off easy. But you've got to stop carrying all of this alone. You're not the only one who's afraid of screwing up."

She looked away, her jaw tight. "It's not the same, Kael. You don't know what it's like to be the one everyone looks to. The one who's supposed to have the answers—and then to lose everything because you didn't."

Kael reached out, gripping her shoulder firmly. "Maybe not in the same way, but I know what it's like to feel like you're not enough. To carry the weight of people you've lost because of your choices. That's why I'm here. That's why I'm standing next to you. You don't have to face this alone."

Her eyes flicked to his, searching for any sign of doubt. When she found none, her shoulders sagged slightly. "You make it sound so simple."

"It's not," Kael admitted. "But it's better than shutting yourself off from everyone. Better than letting this place win."

The ground beneath them trembled slightly, and the ghostly figures turned to face the fractured monument. The woman Lira had been watching raised her hands, and a soundless scream tore through the air, shaking the ruins.

The vision dimmed, the shadows closing in again, and the courtyard reformed around them. Lira let out a shaky breath, her hand releasing the talisman.

"It's like it... heard me," she said, her voice trembling. "Like the city knows what I'm afraid of."

Kael nodded. "Maybe it does. But that doesn't mean it gets to define you. We're not done here, Lira. Not by a long shot. And we're facing this together."

For the first time, she allowed herself a faint smile. "You really don't know when to quit, do you?"

Kael smirked. "Not when it comes to keeping you alive."

Lira shook her head, her smile growing just slightly. "Alright. Together, then."

As they readied themselves to press on, the bond between them felt stronger than ever. The city had tried to break them, to pit them against their fears and regrets. But in the shared struggle, they found something Varunel hadn't accounted for: a partnership built on trust and resilience.

Whatever lay ahead, they would face it together.

Chapter 10
Bonds in the Darkness

The passage opened into a massive plaza, its vastness disorienting after the narrow tunnels. The air here was heavier, each breath coming with effort. The ground beneath them pulsed faintly, a steady rhythm that matched the ominous heartbeat they could feel reverberating in their chests.

Kael stopped in his tracks, scanning the plaza. "Do you feel that?"

"How could I not?" Lira replied, her voice sharp with tension. She tightened her grip on the talisman, its glow faint but steady. "It's like the whole place is alive."

Kael nodded, his gaze darting to the shadows that flitted around the edges of the plaza. They weren't just illusions anymore. These figures moved with purpose, their shapes sharper, more defined.

"Keep that talisman close," Kael said, his voice low but firm. "Whatever's going on here, it's getting stronger. I don't trust these things to stay on the edges."

Lira glanced at him, her eyes narrowing. "You think it's going to get worse?"

He met her gaze, his expression grim. "I think we haven't seen the worst of it yet."

As if in answer, one of the apparitions surged forward, its shape shifting into a humanoid form. Its translucent hand grazed the stone at Lira's feet, leaving a deep gouge in its wake.

"That's new," Kael muttered, drawing his blade.

Lira stepped back, her heart pounding. "They can touch things now?"

"Looks like it," Kael said, positioning himself between Lira and the advancing figure. He held his weapon at the ready, the blade glinting faintly in the dim light. "We're not just fighting memories anymore. These things are real now."

The apparition hissed, its form flickering like a flame in the wind. Lira raised the talisman instinctively, and its glow flared, sending the figure retreating with an unearthly screech.

Kael exhaled sharply. "Okay, that's good to know. The talisman works—at least for now."

"For now," Lira echoed, her grip tightening on the artifact.

The ground beneath them pulsed harder, the heartbeat growing louder. It wasn't just a sound; it was a force, shaking the stones and making the shadows ripple.

Kael glanced around, his voice urgent. "We can't stay here. The plaza's too open, too exposed. If this is Varunel's heart, it's not going to let us hang around without a fight."

Lira nodded, her eyes scanning the area. "But where do we go? The map's useless, and there's no clear path."

"Then we make our own," Kael said, gripping his blade tighter. "We move toward whatever's causing that heartbeat. If it's alive, it can be stopped."

"You make it sound so simple," Lira said, her tone laced with dry humor despite the tension.

Kael gave her a faint grin. "Hey, I'm trying to stay positive. You should try it sometime."

Before Lira could respond, another apparition lunged at them. This one was faster, its clawed hand swiping dangerously close to Kael's side. He dodged, slashing at the figure, but his blade passed through it harmlessly.

"Not so simple," he muttered, retreating toward Lira.

She raised the talisman again, its glow forcing the creature back. "We need to move—now," she said, her voice steady despite the chaos.

Kael nodded, falling into step beside her. "Stick together. Whatever happens, we don't split up."

"Agreed," Lira said, glancing at him. "And if I tell you to run, you run. Got it?"

Kael snorted. "Not a chance. If we're doing this, we're doing it together."

They moved carefully across the plaza, the ground shaking beneath their feet with each pulse. The apparitions circled them, their movements more deliberate now, as though testing the limits of the talisman's protection.

"How much longer do you think this thing will hold them off?" Lira asked, holding the artifact close.

"No idea," Kael admitted. "But as long as it does, we keep moving."

The plaza seemed endless, its boundaries stretching far into the shadows. The pulsing heartbeat grew louder, its rhythm almost deafening now. Lira could feel it in her chest, each beat like a hammer against her ribs.

"We're getting close," Kael said, his voice barely audible over the sound.

"Close to what?" Lira asked, her tone wary.

Kael glanced at her, his expression determined. "To whatever's at the center of all this. The thing that doesn't want us to leave."

Lira's grip on the talisman tightened as they pressed forward, the apparitions growing bolder with each step. Whatever lay at the heart of Varunel, they were about to face it head-on. Together.

The plaza's oppressive silence was broken by the faint sound of footsteps echoing from somewhere ahead. Lira and Kael stopped, their eyes scanning the dimly lit expanse. From the shadows, a figure emerged, cloaked in the familiar deep green robes of Elder Thorne.

Kael tightened his grip on his blade. "This can't be real," he muttered, his tone edged with suspicion.

"Or it's exactly what the city wants us to see," Lira replied, holding the talisman tightly.

The figure approached slowly, her movements deliberate and calm. As she stepped into the faint glow of their lantern, Elder Thorne's face became visible, serene yet solemn.

"You've come far," she said, her voice carrying an ethereal echo that seemed to blend with the whispers of the city. "But your journey is not over."

Lira narrowed her eyes. "Is it really you, or is this another one of Varunel's tricks?"

Thorne tilted her head, a faint smile on her lips. "Does it matter? My presence here serves a purpose, real or not. You've entered the city's heart, and it's time you understood what you're facing."

Kael stepped forward, his tone skeptical. "Alright, then. Explain. What is this place really? And why do these artifacts feel like they're failing us?"

Thorne's gaze swept over them both, her expression unreadable. "Varunel is not just a cursed city. It is a living entity, feeding on the memories of those who enter its boundaries. It absorbs their fears, their regrets, their pain, and weaves them into its fabric. Every shadow, every whisper you've encountered, is a fragment of someone who came before you."

Lira tightened her grip on the talisman, her voice sharp. "And the artifacts? What are they, really? You told us they'd protect us, but they're barely holding up."

Thorne nodded. "They are crafted from the same memories Varunel seeks to consume. Fragments of those who lived here, those who fought against the city's pull. Their power is strongest in places where Varunel's influence is weakest—where the memories they're tied to still hold some semblance of strength."

Kael frowned, his mind racing. "So, what happens when we're in the heart of the city? The artifacts weaken because this is where Varunel is strongest?"

"Precisely," Thorne said, her voice tinged with regret. "The closer you come to the core, the more Varunel asserts its dominance. The artifacts can guide you, but they cannot protect you from everything."

Lira took a step closer, her voice low but intense. "And what happens if we fail? What happens to us if the city gets what it wants?"

Thorne's gaze softened, a hint of sorrow in her eyes. "You become part of it. Your memories, your essence, will join the countless others that Varunel has claimed. You will live on as whispers, as shadows, endlessly replaying the moments that define you."

Kael exchanged a look with Lira, tension thick in the air. "That's why it knows so much about us," he said. "It's been digging into our minds, pulling out what hurts the most."

Thorne nodded. "Yes. And the more you give in to fear, the stronger its hold becomes."

Lira's voice shook slightly as she asked, "Then why send us here? If you knew the artifacts weren't enough, why let us walk into this trap?"

Thorne's expression grew somber. "Because Varunel must be confronted. It cannot be allowed to spread its influence beyond these walls. You have the strength to challenge it—if you can hold on to who you are."

Kael shook his head, frustration clear in his voice. "You could've told us all of this before we came here. Why wait until now?"

Thorne's gaze held steady. "You would not have understood. Some truths must be experienced to be believed."

Lira clenched her fists, her voice bitter. "And if we don't make it out? We just become part of your little memory experiment?"

Thorne stepped closer, her tone firm but gentle. "Your fate is not yet sealed. The city can be resisted, but only if you trust each other—and yourselves. Your bond is your greatest weapon."

Kael glanced at Lira, then back at Thorne. "So, what now? How do we stop this thing?"

Thorne gestured toward the pulsating ground beneath them. "You must reach the core, the very heart of Varunel. Confront it directly. The city will try to break you, to twist your memories against you. But if you stay true to who you are, you can sever its hold."

Lira stared at the elder, her skepticism dimmed but not entirely gone. "And if we succeed?"

"The city's curse will weaken," Thorne said. "Its grip on those trapped here will falter. But you must act quickly. Varunel knows you're here, and it will not let you leave easily."

The elder's form began to fade, her voice echoing around them. "Remember, the city feeds on doubt and fear. Hold fast to your purpose. Trust in each other."

As Thorne vanished completely, the plaza returned to its oppressive silence. Lira turned to Kael, her expression grim but resolute.

"Well," she said, gripping the talisman tightly. "No pressure, right?"

Kael gave a wry smile, his blade at the ready. "None at all. Let's finish this."

Together, they stepped forward, their resolve steeled against the growing darkness. The heart of Varunel awaited.

The rhythmic thrum beneath their feet grew louder as they moved deeper into the labyrinthine pathways. The plaza's oppressive energy gave way to a narrow corridor, its walls etched with faintly glowing runes. Each step felt heavier, as though the air itself were thickening around them.

Kael glanced at Lira, who was holding the map in one hand and the talisman in the other. The map's faintly glowing symbols pulsed irregularly, flickering like a dying flame.

"Are you sure about this?" Kael asked, his voice tense but steady. "Thorne's explanation made it clear these things aren't infallible. What if it's leading us in circles?"

Lira shot him a look, though her usual sharpness was absent. "It's all we have, Kael. If the map still has any power left, we have to trust it. For now."

Kael sighed, glancing at the darkened passage ahead. "Right. For now. Let's hope it doesn't get us killed."

They pressed forward, the glowing symbols on the map fading with every step. Lira's fingers traced the edges of the parchment, her brow furrowed in concentration.

"It's changing," she muttered.

Kael leaned over to look. "Changing how?"

"The lines—they're breaking apart," Lira said, her voice tinged with frustration. "It's like the city is unraveling its guidance as we get closer to the core."

Kael frowned. "Or maybe it's forcing us to stop relying on it."

Lira glanced at him, the skepticism in her gaze tempered by the faintest hint of agreement. "You think this is deliberate? Varunel's way of testing us?"

Kael shrugged, his grip tightening on his blade. "Wouldn't be the first time. This place seems to thrive on making things harder than they need to be."

The map flickered one last time, its glowing lines dissolving into nothingness. The parchment crumbled in Lira's hands, the fragments scattering like ash. She stared at the empty space where the map had been, her lips pressed into a thin line.

"That's it," she said quietly. "We're on our own now."

Kael stepped closer, his voice calm but firm. "No, we're not. We've got everything we need. Thorne said it herself—the artifacts were just tools. The real strength comes from us."

Lira turned to him, her expression hard but thoughtful. "You make it sound so simple. What if that's just her way of saying, 'Good luck, you're on your own'?"

Kael smiled faintly. "Then we prove her wrong."

He took a deep breath, his eyes fixed on the path ahead. "Let's focus on what we're here to do. We stop Varunel's curse. We sever its connection to all the people it's taken. That's the mission."

Lira nodded slowly, her grip tightening on the talisman. "And for me... it's about more than the mission. This city has taken too much from too many. If stopping it means facing everything I've been running from, then that's what I'll do."

Kael gave her an encouraging nod. "That's the spirit. We've made it this far, haven't we?"

"Just barely," Lira muttered, though her tone lacked its usual edge.

They continued down the corridor, the pulse beneath their feet growing stronger. The glow from the runes on the walls dimmed as they moved forward, replaced by an eerie darkness that seemed to press in on them from all sides.

Kael broke the silence, his voice steady. "So, what's your plan when this is all over? Assuming we make it out of here alive."

Lira glanced at him, a flicker of amusement crossing her face. "I haven't thought that far ahead. Surviving Varunel seems like enough of a challenge for now."

"Fair point," Kael said with a chuckle. "But if we do make it out, you should think about taking some time off. Maybe somewhere sunny. You know, far away from cursed cities."

Lira snorted, the sound almost a laugh. "I'll consider it. What about you?"

Kael shrugged. "Maybe I'll write a book. 'How Not to Die in a Haunted City.' Could be a bestseller."

"Catchy title," Lira said dryly. "You'd better survive to write it, then."

"That's the plan," Kael replied, his grin fading as the corridor widened into another chamber.

The heartbeat beneath their feet was deafening now, the air vibrating with its rhythm. Lira took a steadying breath, her gaze hardening as she looked at Kael.

"Whatever's ahead, we face it together," she said.

"Together," Kael echoed, stepping beside her.

As they stepped into the chamber, the oppressive darkness gave way to an ominous glow emanating from its center. The core of Varunel awaited them, and there was no turning back.

The chamber was alive. Mist coiled and writhed around their feet, thick and heavy like a physical weight pressing against their chests. The glow at the center of the room pulsed with a steady rhythm, casting flickering shadows that danced across the cracked walls. The voices were no longer whispers but a cacophony of sound—words overlapping and weaving together into a suffocating tapestry of fear and desire.

Kael stopped, his hand tightening around his blade. "It's louder here," he said, his voice raised to cut through the noise.

Lira nodded, her grip firm on the talisman. "It's more than that. It's... pulling. I can feel it."

Kael turned to her, his face tense. "Pulling how? What do you mean?"

She swallowed hard, her eyes darting toward the glowing center of the room. "It's like it knows me. It's not just fear anymore—it's offering something. Promises. Lies, maybe, but..."

"But they feel real," Kael finished for her.

She met his gaze, her expression a mix of anger and vulnerability. "Exactly. It's like it's trying to fill the cracks, patch over everything I've lost. Part of me wants to believe it."

"Lira," Kael said, stepping closer, his voice firm but kind. "That's what it does. It digs into you, finds your weaknesses, and exploits them. You can't give it that power."

Her jaw tightened. "I know that. But knowing doesn't make it easier."

The voices surged, one louder than the rest—a voice that sounded like Lira's father.

"Lira... come home. It's safe here."

She froze, her eyes widening. "No. That's not..."

Kael grabbed her arm, grounding her. "Lira, focus. It's not him. It's the city."

The mist swirled around her feet, rising to her knees. She clenched her fists, her breathing shallow. "It feels real, Kael. Too real."

Kael's voice was sharp. "Then we remind it who we are. That's how we win."

"How?" she asked, her voice trembling.

"By refusing to let it define us," Kael said. He gestured toward the glowing center. "That thing—whatever it is—it thrives on our doubts. You've been facing yours this whole time. Don't stop now."

Lira let out a shaky laugh, her lips curling into a bitter smile. "Easy for you to say. You've always been the optimist."

Kael smirked. "It's a lot harder than it looks. Trust me."

The mist thickened, rising higher, and the voices grew louder. Kael's own name echoed through the chamber, the voice eerily familiar.

"Kael... you could've saved us. Why didn't you?"

He stiffened, his expression hardening. "Not real," he muttered to himself. "Not this time."

Lira noticed his hesitation and stepped closer. "Kael. Don't let it in. You've been pulling me through this, but you can't carry both of us."

He shook his head, his voice low. "It's nothing. Just... old ghosts."

She gripped his arm, forcing him to look at her. "Don't lie to me. If we're doing this, we do it together. You told me that."

Kael met her gaze, the tension in his shoulders easing slightly. "You're right. Together."

The voices around them shifted, merging into a single entity. It spoke with a deep, resonant tone that seemed to vibrate through the chamber.

"You cannot resist. I am everything you fear, everything you desire. You belong to me."

Lira raised the talisman, its glow faint but steady. Her voice was strong despite the tremor in her hands. "You're wrong. I've spent too long letting fear control me. I won't do it anymore."

Kael stepped beside her, his blade raised. "And I've spent too long running from my failures. Not today."

The mist swirled violently, the pulse of the glowing core growing erratic. The air seemed to crackle with energy, the city reacting to their defiance.

Lira glanced at Kael, her expression resolute. "We end this. No more running, no more hiding."

Kael nodded, his grip tightening on his blade. "No more. Whatever happens, we face it head-on."

The two of them stepped forward, their resolve solidified as the voices screamed in protest. The core of Varunel awaited, and they were ready to confront it together.

Chapter 11
The Waking Curse

The chamber was vast and circular, its walls pulsating with an unnatural, dim light that seemed to emanate from the very air. The floor beneath Lira and Kael felt uneven, shifting subtly as if alive. The heart of Varunel pulsed louder here, its rhythm syncing with their racing hearts.

Kael stopped, gripping his blade tightly. "This is it. The heart of the city."

"Feels more like the stomach," Lira muttered, her voice tense but steady.

The moment they stepped further inside, the air thickened, and shadows began to form around them. These weren't like the fleeting apparitions they'd encountered before. These figures were sharper, more defined, with faces that sent chills through their spines.

Lira froze as a figure stepped forward from the mist. It was a tall, stern-faced man, his eyes piercing even in the dim glow. His cloak was tattered, but the insignia of her old guild was unmistakable on his chest.

"Master Evarin," Lira whispered, her voice faltering.

The apparition tilted its head, its expression unreadable. When it spoke, the voice was his—but layered with something darker. "You let us fall, Lira. Your arrogance destroyed everything we built."

Kael stepped closer, his blade at the ready. "Lira, it's not him. Don't let it get to you."

"I know it's not him," she snapped, though her eyes remained locked on the figure. "But it doesn't make it any easier."

Evarin's apparition stepped closer, his form flickering but his voice steady. "You were supposed to lead. You were supposed to protect. But you were too stubborn to listen. Too weak to admit you needed help."

"That's enough!" Lira shouted, her hands trembling as she gripped the talisman.

Kael turned, his jaw tightening as another figure emerged from the mist—this one smaller, slighter. It was a boy, no older than fifteen, with wide, terrified eyes. Kael's breath caught in his throat.

"No," he muttered, shaking his head.

The boy took a step forward, his movements halting and unnatural. "You left me, Kael," the figure said, its voice trembling with a mix of fear and accusation. "You promised you'd come back. But you didn't."

Kael's grip on his blade faltered. "I didn't have a choice," he said, his voice low, almost pleading. "I couldn't save everyone."

"But you could've saved me," the boy replied, his voice cutting through the air like a knife.

Lira turned to Kael, her own turmoil momentarily forgotten. "Kael, don't let it in. You told me that, remember?"

He clenched his jaw, nodding. "I'm trying," he said, his voice strained.

The apparitions moved closer, their forms more solid with each step. The air between them seemed to shimmer, charged with the weight of memories too painful to bear.

Evarin's voice grew sharper. "You've never been enough, Lira. And you never will be."

Kael's shadowed boy mirrored the sentiment. "You left me. And now you'll leave her too."

"No!" Lira shouted, the talisman in her hand flaring to life. Its light pushed the apparitions back momentarily, giving them a brief reprieve. She turned to Kael, her voice firm despite the fear in her eyes. "This is what the city does. It's trying to break us, Kael. We can't let it."

Kael exhaled slowly, his grip on his blade steadying. "You're right. It's not real. It's just noise."

Lira nodded, her gaze returning to Evarin's apparition. "You're not him," she said, her voice cold. "And you don't define me anymore."

The figure faltered, its edges blurring.

Kael stepped forward, facing the boy. "And I don't owe you anything," he said, his voice resolute. "I've made my peace with what happened. You're not going to use it against me."

The mist thickened again, the apparitions writhing as though the defiance had wounded them. The heart of Varunel pulsed louder, the ground beneath their feet trembling.

Lira looked at Kael, her expression fierce. "Whatever's next, we face it together."

Kael nodded, his jaw set. "Together."

They stepped forward into the heart of the city, leaving the ghosts of their pasts behind. The pulse grew louder, the final confrontation drawing near.

The mist thickened around them, twisting and writhing like living tendrils. Every step forward seemed harder, as though the air itself resisted their movement. Lira gritted her teeth, her breaths coming in shallow gasps as the mist coiled tighter around her legs, dragging her pace to a crawl.

Kael glanced over his shoulder, his expression grim. "It's not just mist anymore. It's... something else."

"It's the city," Lira said, her voice tight. "It's reacting to us, to how we feel. The more I push, the more it pushes back."

Kael turned back to her, his brow furrowing. "Then stop pushing. You can't fight this like it's something solid."

"Easy for you to say," she snapped, though her voice lacked venom. Her hands clenched into fists at her sides, trembling slightly. "You're not the one it's targeting."

Kael paused, stepping closer to her. The mist surged between them as though trying to keep them apart, forming a wall of shimmering gray. He pushed through it, his hand gripping her shoulder firmly.

"Hey," he said, his tone steady. "Don't give it that power. This thing feeds on fear, on doubt. If you let it, it'll drown you in your own head."

Lira's jaw tightened, her gaze dropping to the swirling mist at her feet. "I know that. But knowing doesn't make it stop. It's like it knows exactly what to show me, what to make me feel."

Kael crouched slightly to meet her eye level, his voice softening. "Then stop letting it dictate the terms. If it's reflecting your emotions, use that. Calm your breathing, focus on something real—something outside of all this."

Lira let out a shaky laugh, though there was no humor in it. "Something real? Like what? The ground that feels like it's breathing, or the walls that are probably watching us?"

Kael smiled faintly. "Me. Focus on me. I'm pretty real, last I checked."

She met his gaze, her lips pressing into a thin line. "You're infuriating, you know that?"

"Part of my charm," he replied, his tone light but his grip steady.

Lira inhaled deeply, forcing herself to focus on his face. The mist around them seemed to hesitate, its swirling slowing as her breathing steadied.

"There you go," Kael said encouragingly. "It's just a city. A really creepy, cursed city, sure, but it's still just a city. You've faced worse."

"Have I?" she asked, raising an eyebrow.

He chuckled. "You've faced me. That's saying something."

Despite herself, Lira smirked. The tension in her shoulders eased slightly, and the mist around her legs loosened its grip.

"See? You're doing it," Kael said, his voice carrying a confidence she envied.

Lira glanced around, noticing how the mist still seemed to form walls, blocking paths and herding them forward. "It's not letting us choose where to go," she said, her tone calmer now.

Kael stood straight, his hand dropping back to his side. "Then we go where it wants us to. For now. It's trying to control us, but that only works if we let it."

"You think it's that simple?" Lira asked, her skepticism returning.

"No," Kael admitted. "But I think our best chance is sticking together and keeping this thing from driving us apart."

She studied him for a moment, then nodded. "Alright. Together, then. But don't expect me to get all philosophical about this."

"Wouldn't dream of it," he said with a grin.

As they moved forward, the mist shifted but didn't press as hard against them. Lira could feel the city's influence still tugging at her mind, but Kael's presence grounded her. The connection they'd built over their journey felt like a lifeline, one that Varunel couldn't sever.

Each step brought them closer to the heart of the city, the oppressive pulse growing louder, but their resolve felt stronger. Whatever Varunel had left to throw at them, they were ready to face it—together.

The chamber's glow dimmed as the pulsing heartbeat of the city reached a deafening crescendo. From the swirling mist at the center, a towering figure began to take shape. It was massive, its form ever-shifting, composed of countless faces that emerged and disappeared into the haze. Eyes filled with sorrow and mouths twisted in anguish covered its surface, whispering fragments of memories and regrets.

Kael tightened his grip on his blade, his jaw clenched. "Well, that's new."

Lira stood frozen, her gaze locked on the apparition. The talisman in her hand flickered weakly, its light barely illuminating the oppressive darkness around them.

"It's not just one spirit," she said, her voice barely audible. "It's all of them. Everything Varunel has taken."

The apparition's hollow eyes turned toward them, its gaze piercing. Its voices rose into a dissonant chorus, each word a blend of pain and accusation.

"You cannot escape. You are part of us now."

Lira's knees buckled slightly, the weight of the voices pressing down on her like a physical force. Memories she'd buried began to surface—her mentor's disappointed gaze, the screams of her comrades, the suffocating guilt of her past failures.

"Lira!" Kael's voice cut through the noise, grounding her. He stepped closer, his hand brushing against her arm. "Stay with me. This thing feeds on fear. Don't let it pull you under."

She shook her head, her breathing ragged. "It's too much, Kael. I can feel it—everything I've tried to forget. Everything I've tried to be stronger than."

He turned to face her fully, his tone steady but urgent. "You are strong, Lira. But strength doesn't mean ignoring what's inside you. It's facing it, even when it feels impossible."

The apparition loomed closer, tendrils of mist lashing out toward them. Kael swung his blade, the steel passing harmlessly through the vapor.

"Great," he muttered. "Looks like it's up to the talisman."

Lira tightened her grip on the artifact, but its glow faltered. "It's almost out of power," she said, panic creeping into her voice.

"Then we make the last of it count," Kael said. He stepped in front of her, his shoulders squared. "Together, remember? We face it together."

The apparition lunged, its massive form bearing down on them. Lira raised the talisman instinctively, its faint light expanding just enough to push the entity back. But the effort left her trembling, the artifact's glow flickering dangerously low.

The apparition's voices surged, one louder than the rest. It spoke directly to Lira, its tone filled with venom.

"You hide behind strength, but you are hollow. You will fail again, as you always have."

Lira's breath caught in her throat, her hands shaking.

Kael turned to her, his voice firm. "Don't listen to it. That's not you. It's just fear trying to control you."

"But what if it's right?" she whispered, her voice cracking. "What if all of this—everything I've done—it's just been a way to hide from the truth? I'm not strong. I've just been too scared to admit I'm not."

Kael stepped closer, his hand gripping her shoulder tightly. "You're wrong, Lira. You're one of the strongest people I know—not because you've been stoic, but because you've kept going, even when it's hurt. That's what real strength is."

The apparition lashed out again, its tendrils slicing through the air. Kael raised his blade in a futile attempt to block it, but the talisman flared once more, its light forming a protective barrier around them.

Lira stared at the artifact, her resolve hardening. "You're right. I've been using my walls as a crutch, pretending that ignoring my fear would make it disappear. But it doesn't."

She stepped forward, holding the talisman high. Its light grew brighter, feeding off her renewed determination. "I'm done running from it," she said, her voice clear and strong. "You want my fear? You can have it. But it won't stop me."

The apparition recoiled, its form flickering as the talisman's glow intensified.

Kael grinned, his confidence bolstered by her resolve. "That's more like it."

With one final surge of light, the talisman unleashed its remaining energy, forcing the apparition back. The faces on its surface screamed in unison before dissolving into the mist, which began to dissipate into nothingness.

The chamber fell silent, the oppressive weight lifting from the air. Lira lowered the talisman, its glow extinguished, and turned to Kael.

"It's gone," she said, her voice quiet but steady.

"For now," Kael replied, sheathing his blade. "But we're still here. And we're still us."

Lira allowed herself a faint smile. "Together, then."

"Always," Kael said, his grin returning.

As they stood in the now-empty chamber, the heartbeat of Varunel faded into silence. The city's core had been confronted, and they had survived—not by avoiding their fears, but by facing them head-on, together.

The chamber trembled as the apparition writhed in pain, its massive form flickering like a dying flame. The faces on its surface screamed, their cries overlapping in a cacophony of anguish. The mist that had once choked the room began to thin, revealing cracks in the floor and walls where faint light seeped through.

Kael stood steady, his blade at his side, his focus on Lira as she clutched the now-dim talisman. "It's working," he said, his voice loud enough to carry over the noise. "You're breaking it, Lira!"

She didn't respond immediately, her gaze fixed on the apparition as it twisted and thrashed. Her hands were trembling, but her expression was calm—resolute.

Kael stepped closer, his voice softer. "You're stronger than it, Lira. You've proven that. Just a little more."

She exhaled sharply, nodding. "It's not just me. We did this together. I couldn't have made it here alone."

Kael smirked. "Team effort, huh? I'll take that."

The apparition surged forward one last time, its form collapsing inward as though it were imploding. Its voice rose in a desperate wail. *"You will never be free! You are nothing without me!"*

Lira stepped forward, her voice firm. "You're wrong. I've been something without you this entire time. I just didn't realize it." She raised the talisman high, its faint light sparking back to life.

Kael moved to stand beside her. "And we're leaving. Together. You don't control us anymore."

The light from the talisman spread outward, flooding the chamber with a warm, golden glow. The apparition shattered like glass, its fragments dissolving into the thinning mist. The walls stopped pulsing, the tremors beneath their feet ceased, and the oppressive weight in the air vanished.

The mist lifted entirely, revealing a clear path leading out of the chamber. Kael turned to Lira, a wide grin on his face. "That's it. We did it."

Lira let out a shaky laugh, lowering the talisman. "We actually did it."

Kael offered a hand. "Come on. Let's get out of here before the city changes its mind."

She hesitated for only a moment before taking his hand. "You're not going to let me hear the end of this, are you?"

Kael chuckled as they began walking. "Not a chance. You've officially joined the 'Kael was right' club. Membership benefits include relentless teasing and occasional motivational speeches."

Lira rolled her eyes, though a small smile tugged at her lips. "I'll pass on the speeches, thanks."

The path led them through the ruins of Varunel, now eerily quiet. The oppressive whispers and flickering shadows were gone, replaced by a strange stillness.

Kael broke the silence first. "So, what now? Back to the guild? Or are you thinking of retiring to some peaceful village where nobody's trying to kill you?"

Lira snorted. "Peaceful doesn't suit me. But... maybe I'll take a break. Reassess things." She glanced at him, her expression softening. "What about you? Going to write that book you mentioned?"

Kael grinned. "'How Not to Die in a Haunted City'? Absolutely. Chapter one: Always bring a Lira. Turns out they're pretty handy in a pinch."

She smirked, shaking her head. "You're insufferable."

"And yet, you're still here," he shot back with a wink.

They reached the city's edge as the first rays of sunlight pierced the horizon. The ruins behind them seemed less menacing in the light, almost peaceful.

Lira stopped, turning to look back at Varunel. "It feels... different now. Like it's finally at rest."

Kael nodded, his tone serious for once. "We gave it what it needed—closure. And maybe we found some of that for ourselves, too."

She met his gaze, her voice softer. "I think you're right. About that, at least."

He grinned. "I'll take it."

They turned and began walking away from the city, the weight of their shared experience settling into something lighter. Whatever challenges lay ahead, they knew they could face them—together.

For the first time in a long time, Lira felt something unfamiliar: peace. And as they left Varunel behind, she realized that facing her fears hadn't just weakened the city's curse—it had freed her as well.

Chapter 12
Truth in the Shadows

The ruins of Varunel stretched out behind them, the once-oppressive shadows now fading in the soft light of dawn. The air felt lighter with every step they took away from the city, as if its grip on them was finally loosening.

Kael glanced over his shoulder, his voice breaking the silence. "You feel that? It's like we can actually breathe again."

Lira nodded, her gaze fixed on the path ahead. "It's quieter. Like the city's finally... letting go."

Kael smirked. "I didn't think cities could hold grudges, but this one sure gave it a good shot."

Lira let out a short laugh, surprising herself. "It did, didn't it? But it wasn't just the city, Kael. It was us, too—everything we brought in with us."

Kael raised an eyebrow. "You're saying Varunel just amplified what was already there?"

"Exactly," Lira said, glancing at him. "It used our fears against us, but those fears were ours to begin with. We gave it the ammunition."

Kael nodded thoughtfully. "And here I was, thinking we'd just walked into the worst haunted house in existence."

"It was more than that," Lira said, her tone quieter now. "It forced us to look at things we've been running from. Things I've been running from."

Kael slowed his pace, turning to face her. "You really think you've been running? You don't strike me as the 'run away' type."

She met his gaze, her expression softer than he was used to. "Not physically, no. But emotionally? Definitely. I've spent so long pretending I had everything under control, like admitting I was scared would somehow make me weaker."

Kael tilted his head, a faint smile tugging at his lips. "And now?"

"Now I know better," she said, her voice steady. "It's not about ignoring fear. It's about moving forward anyway, even when it feels impossible."

Kael nodded, his expression thoughtful. "That's a good way to look at it. I think I've been the opposite, though. Too curious for my own good, always poking at things I didn't understand."

"Like cursed cities?" Lira said, a smirk playing on her lips.

He laughed. "Exactly. But this trip? It's made me realize there's more to the supernatural than just curiosity. Respect, I guess. For what it represents—and for what it can teach us."

Lira's expression softened. "You've changed, too, Kael. A little less reckless, maybe. Or at least, less annoying about it."

"High praise," he said with a grin.

They walked in silence for a few moments, the ruins giving way to open fields bathed in soft morning light. The oppressive weight they'd carried since entering Varunel was gone, replaced by a strange sense of peace.

Kael broke the quiet, his voice reflective. "You think we'll ever come back here?"

Lira shook her head. "I don't need to. Varunel doesn't hold anything for me anymore. It was never about the city—it was about what it forced me to face."

He nodded. "Fair enough. But I'll admit, part of me is still curious about what else might be hiding in there."

She raised an eyebrow. "You really are impossible."

"Hey," he said, throwing up his hands defensively. "Curiosity is a strength. You said it yourself—moving forward even when it feels impossible."

Lira smirked. "I'm pretty sure I wasn't talking about running headfirst into another cursed city."

Kael grinned. "Details."

They reached the edge of the ruins, where the path turned into a familiar trail that would lead them back to safety. Lira stopped, looking back at the ruins one last time.

"Goodbye, Varunel," she said softly, her voice carrying a mixture of relief and closure.

Kael placed a hand on her shoulder. "Goodbye, ghosts. Don't come looking for us."

They turned and continued down the trail, the light growing stronger with every step. For the first time in what felt like an eternity, they were free—not just from the city, but from the weight of their own pasts.

Their journey wasn't over, but they walked forward with a newfound sense of purpose. Together.

The Veiled Gates stood before them, towering and ancient, their intricate carvings shimmering faintly in the morning light. The oppressive mist that had once cloaked this threshold was gone, replaced by a serene stillness that felt almost reverent.

Kael paused, his gaze sweeping over the carvings. "I never thought these gates could look... peaceful."

Lira nodded, her hand brushing against the talisman at her side. It was silent now, its glow extinguished, but she still felt its presence, like a faint hum of reassurance.

As they stepped closer, a figure materialized from the shadows, her green robes unmistakable even in the soft light. Elder Thorne stood before them, her expression calm but knowing.

"You've done well," Thorne said, her voice carrying the weight of centuries.

Lira crossed her arms, her tone skeptical but not unkind. "You always seem to show up at just the right moment. Almost like you planned it."

Thorne allowed a small smile. "I didn't plan your path, Lira. The city did. My role was simply to prepare you for the truth."

Kael raised an eyebrow. "The truth? That Varunel isn't just cursed—it's a cycle?"

Thorne inclined her head. "Precisely. Varunel is not merely a city. It is a mirror, reflecting the souls of those who enter. Its curse lies in its ability to feed on the fears, regrets, and unspoken truths of those who cannot confront themselves. Only outsiders—those untouched by the city's origins—can hope to weaken its hold."

Lira's brow furrowed, her voice quieter now. "And by confronting our own fears, we broke part of that cycle?"

"You have weakened its grasp," Thorne confirmed. "Varunel will remain, for now. But its power diminishes each time someone emerges with their soul intact. You have shown it what it cannot take from you."

Kael frowned, his curiosity still burning. "But why us? Why send us in with artifacts that barely held up? Why not warn us about everything we'd face?"

Thorne's gaze was steady, her voice tinged with both wisdom and regret. "Because knowing too much would have made you vulnerable. You needed to discover your strength through the journey itself. The artifacts were never meant to save you—they were tools to guide you, nothing more."

Lira exhaled slowly, the weight of Thorne's words settling over her. "So this was always about us. Not the city."

"Both," Thorne said. "You cannot separate Varunel's curse from its victims. It is a symbiosis, one that thrives on unresolved truths. By confronting your own, you've weakened the cycle."

Kael tilted his head, his expression thoughtful. "And what about you, Thorne? You've been here for... how long? How do you fit into all of this?"

Thorne's smile was faint, almost wistful. "My role is to guide those who enter, to show them the path to their own truths. It is not my curse to break. That lies with those who still carry the weight of the living world."

Lira met Thorne's gaze, her tone softening. "Thank you. For what you've done. I didn't see it before, but... I get it now. We needed this. I needed this."

Thorne inclined her head, her expression warm. "You are welcome, Lira. And you, Kael. Your bond has carried you farther than either of you might have walked alone. That, too, is part of the lesson."

Kael smirked, glancing at Lira. "Hear that? We're a team. Guess you're stuck with me now."

Lira rolled her eyes, though her faint smile betrayed her amusement. "Don't push your luck."

Thorne stepped back, her form already beginning to fade. "The path beyond the gates is yours. Walk it well, and remember—Varunel is not gone. But it is weaker because of you."

As her figure dissolved into the morning light, the Veiled Gates creaked open, revealing the rolling fields beyond. Kael turned to Lira, his voice lighter now. "Ready to leave this place behind?"

Lira nodded, her grip on the talisman loosening as she took her first step forward. "More than ready. Let's go."

They passed through the gates together, the weight of Varunel's curse lifting with each step. The lessons of the city lingered, etched into their hearts, but the bond they'd forged gave them the strength to carry those truths into whatever lay ahead.

For the first time, the horizon felt open—full of possibility.

The moment they stepped through the Veiled Gates, the atmosphere shifted. The oppressive weight that had followed them since entering Varunel lifted, replaced by a lightness that felt almost foreign. The mist thinned and dissipated, revealing rolling fields bathed in warm sunlight.

Kael stopped just beyond the threshold, tilting his head back to take a deep breath. "It's different out here," he said, his voice quiet. "Almost like we were holding our breath the entire time we were inside."

Lira paused beside him, her eyes scanning the horizon. The edges of her features, often sharp with tension, softened as she exhaled deeply. "It does feel lighter," she admitted.

Kael grinned, though it was tinged with something contemplative. "We made it. We actually made it out."

Lira turned to look at him, raising an eyebrow. "Surprised?"

He chuckled, rubbing the back of his neck. "A little. If you'd told me when we first got here that we'd be walking out in one piece, I might've called you crazy."

Her smirk was faint but genuine. "Good thing I didn't make any promises."

They began walking down the narrow trail leading away from the gates, their footsteps muffled by the soft grass beneath them. The ruins of Varunel loomed quietly behind them, still vast and foreboding, but now more distant and less threatening.

Kael broke the silence first, his tone reflective. "You know, part of me... I don't know. I can't shake the feeling that we just scratched the surface back there. Like there's more to Varunel than we ever really understood."

Lira shot him a glance, her skepticism evident. "You want to go back? After everything we just went through?"

He shrugged, his expression thoughtful. "Not now. Maybe not for a long time. But yeah... someday. There are answers in that city, Lira. About the curse, about the people it took. About what it really wants."

Lira's steps slowed slightly, her gaze drifting to the horizon. She didn't reply immediately, her mind turning over his words.

Finally, she said, "You'd have to be even more prepared next time. Smarter. Stronger. Not just running in with a glowing rock and a flimsy map."

Kael laughed, the sound breaking through the lingering tension like sunlight piercing clouds. "Flimsy map? I seem to remember it saving us more than once."

"It also disintegrated," Lira pointed out, though there was no venom in her tone.

Kael nodded, his smile fading into something more subdued. "True. But we didn't need it in the end, did we? We figured it out ourselves."

Lira stopped walking, turning to face him fully. "That's the only reason we're standing here now. Because we stopped relying on things that couldn't carry us the whole way."

Kael met her gaze, a flicker of pride in his eyes. "And maybe that's why we could go back someday. We know what it takes now. We know who we are."

Lira crossed her arms, tilting her head slightly. "Maybe. But for now, I'm more interested in what lies ahead, not what's behind us."

Kael smiled, motioning to the path before them. "Then let's keep moving. Varunel can wait."

As they resumed their journey, the ruins of the city grew smaller in the distance, its shadows no longer reaching for them. The sunlight grew warmer, the air lighter, and for the first time, the weight they'd carried with them for so long felt manageable—shared, rather than borne alone.

Lira glanced back only once, her expression unreadable, before turning her attention to the horizon. Kael, ever curious, lingered for a moment longer, his thoughts already racing with questions he might one day answer.

But for now, they walked forward—changed, but not defined by the past they'd confronted. Together, they stepped into a world that felt brighter, the open road waiting for whatever might come next.

The path leading away from Varunel stretched before them, bathed in golden light. Lira and Kael walked side by side, their steps slow and deliberate, neither in a rush to leave the quiet peace that had settled over them. The weight of the city was gone, replaced by a tangible lightness that neither had felt in years.

Kael broke the silence first, his voice soft but tinged with humor. "So, we survived. Against all odds, I might add. Not bad for two stubborn fools with a glowing rock and a half-baked plan."

Lira smirked, shaking her head. "Don't get too proud of yourself. Half the time, I thought we weren't going to make it."

"Half the time?" Kael shot her a mock-injured look. "You mean I didn't inspire unwavering confidence the entire way?"

She chuckled, the sound rare and genuine. "Let's just say your motivational speeches were... unique. But," she added, her tone softening, "you did help. More than I expected."

Kael grinned, his usual playfulness tempered by sincerity. "I'll take that as a win. And you—you were the rock, Lira. Even when you thought you weren't."

She glanced at him, her brow furrowing slightly. "I spent so much time trying to hide what I was feeling. Pretending I wasn't scared. But it wasn't strength. It was avoidance."

Kael nodded, his expression thoughtful. "And now?"

"Now I know better," she said, her voice steady. "Strength isn't about pretending you're not afraid. It's about facing it anyway. You taught me that."

He raised an eyebrow. "Me? Pretty sure you figured that out on your own."

"Maybe," she said with a faint smile. "But you didn't let me do it alone. That matters."

Kael stopped walking, turning to face her fully. "You didn't let me, either. That city—it dragged everything out of me. Things I'd buried so deep I didn't think they'd ever see the light. But you called me on it. Made me face it."

Lira tilted her head, studying him for a moment. "We made a good team, didn't we?"

"The best," Kael said with a grin.

Ahead of them, the faint silhouette of Elder Thorne appeared, standing at the edge of the path. She watched them approach, her expression calm and knowing.

"You've done well," Thorne said as they reached her. "Both of you."

Lira crossed her arms, a smirk playing on her lips. "You love saying that, don't you?"

Thorne's lips curved into a faint smile. "Because it's true. You have faced what few could and emerged stronger. Varunel will not soon forget you."

Kael frowned slightly, his curiosity sparking again. "So... that's it? We leave, and the city just goes back to waiting for the next poor souls to wander in?"

Thorne's expression grew somber. "Varunel is not easily undone. Its cycle continues, but each crack in its foundation weakens its hold. You have made a difference, even if the city's echoes linger."

Lira nodded, her voice quieter now. "We'll never forget it. But we won't be back."

Thorne inclined her head. "That is as it should be. Your paths lie beyond these gates now, not within them."

Kael hesitated, then offered Thorne a small smile. "Thanks. For what you did. Even if I didn't always understand it, you were... helpful."

Thorne's smile widened slightly. "High praise indeed, Kael. Farewell, both of you. Walk your paths with strength and purpose."

She stepped back, her form dissolving into the morning mist as though she had never been there.

Kael let out a breath, shaking his head. "She really knows how to make an exit."

Lira chuckled, nudging him lightly. "Come on. Let's get moving."

As they continued down the trail, the ruins of Varunel faded behind them. The weight of the city was now just a memory—haunting, yes, but no longer oppressive.

Kael glanced at Lira, his tone light. "Think we'll ever top this adventure?"

She raised an eyebrow. "I hope not. I'm done with cursed cities for a while."

"Fair enough," he said with a grin.

They walked in comfortable silence, the bond forged in Varunel now an unspoken understanding. Their mission was complete, but their personal journeys stretched ahead, full of possibilities they hadn't dared to imagine before.

And for the first time in years, both felt ready to face whatever came next. Together or apart, they carried the strength of their shared experience—and the knowledge that even in the darkest places, there was always a way forward.

Chapter 13
Fractured Souls

They stepped into the hidden chamber, a space concealed within the depths of Varunel, cloaked in shadows so thick it felt as though they were walking into the very heart of the city's curse. A faint, eerie glow lit the room from above, casting long shadows on the walls that seemed to move as they passed, as if the city itself was watching, waiting for their next move.

At the center of the chamber, resting on a pedestal covered in dust and ivy, lay an ancient, worn book. Its cover was cracked and faded, but there was a strange elegance to it, as if it held something sacred within its fragile pages. Lira felt a shiver run down her spine as she approached, the weight of countless memories pressing in on her, making it difficult to breathe.

Kael stepped up beside her, his gaze fixed on the tome. "Do you feel that?" he whispered, his voice low, reverent. "It's like… every story trapped here is woven into this one book."

Lira nodded, reaching out but hesitating just before her fingers touched the cover. "It's more than just a book. It's… it's everything Varunel has taken, every life, every love… every broken heart." She swallowed, her voice dropping. "And it's calling to us."

She opened the cover carefully, the pages whispering as they turned, revealing faded ink and scrawled lines of handwriting that varied from page to page, like voices speaking through time. She read the first line aloud, her voice wavering as the words sank in.

"I vowed to love her until my last breath, but Varunel claimed that vow and twisted it into chains."

Kael's hand rested on the edge of the tome, his gaze intent as he leaned closer. "It's like… each page holds a piece of their souls, their final confessions, their regrets. They all came here for love, and Varunel… trapped them."

He turned to another page, reading aloud, "She left me here, her promises slipping into shadow. And now I wait, hoping to see her face once more, even if it means eternity." His voice faltered, and he looked up, his eyes meeting Lira's. "They're all here, waiting. It's like their stories are woven into the city itself."

Lira's fingers trembled as she turned another page, the words echoing in her mind, each confession a mirror to her own fears. "I held back, afraid of what I might lose, only to lose everything by staying silent." Her voice grew quieter, the words settling heavily in her heart. "They kept their hearts guarded… and it cost them everything."

Kael looked at her, his voice soft but insistent. "Does that sound familiar? All these people, they couldn't move on, couldn't let go of the past, and Varunel… it consumed them. It's using their pain, their regrets, as fuel. But Lira… we don't have to let that happen to us."

She glanced at him, her eyes shadowed with the weight of her own regrets. "And what if it's already happening, Kael? What if, by being here, by holding onto everything, we're becoming just another story in this book? Another warning for the next fool who comes here?"

He reached out, his hand covering hers on the tome, grounding her. "Then maybe this book isn't just a collection of tragedies. Maybe it's a reminder. A way to understand what we're fighting for—and what we need to leave behind."

She closed her eyes, the voices from the book swirling around her, whispers of love and loss, betrayal and longing. Each voice was a fragment of herself, pieces of her own fears reflected back at her, as if Varunel itself was forcing her to confront what she'd spent so long burying.

She turned to another page, reading aloud, her voice thick with emotion. "I was afraid to say what I felt, to admit the depth of what was in my heart. I thought protecting myself would save me… but all it did was leave me alone."

Kael's fingers tightened around hers, his gaze steady. "Lira, these are the words of people who waited too long, who let fear keep them from facing what was real. We're here now. We have a choice to break the pattern."

She shook her head, her voice barely a whisper. "It's not that simple, Kael. I've spent years protecting myself, guarding my heart because I thought it was the only way to survive. How do you just… let that go?"

He looked into her eyes, his voice gentle. "You let it go by trusting. By taking a chance, even if it scares you. By realizing that maybe... maybe love isn't something to be guarded against. Maybe it's what gives us strength, what lets us face the shadows instead of hiding from them."

A silence settled between them, filled with the weight of their shared understanding and the stories that lay between the pages. Lira felt the words resonate within her, each confession from the tome a reminder of everything she feared, and everything she could no longer deny.

Slowly, she closed the book, her hand still resting on its cover, the whispers fading into the mist. She looked up at Kael, a hint of resolve in her gaze, her voice steady but laced with vulnerability. "Then let's make sure we're not just another story in this book, Kael. Let's find a way to break Varunel's hold... together."

His hand stayed on hers, his voice filled with quiet determination. "Together. We won't let this city write our ending."

And as they turned to leave the chamber, the city's shadows seemed to retreat, if only for a moment, as though Varunel itself felt the shift in their hearts—a decision made, a vow of their own, a promise to survive.

They sat beside the Lover's Tome, the weight of the chamber's silence settling over them. The tome lay open between them, its faded pages filled with the confessions and regrets of souls Varunel had ensnared. Kael's hand rested on the book, his fingers tracing the faded ink as if he could feel the emotions woven into each word.

After a long silence, Kael looked at Lira, his voice soft but intent. "Lira... we don't have to be like them. We don't have to let this place use our regrets against us."

She met his gaze, hesitating before letting out a quiet sigh. "It's not that simple, Kael. Sometimes... regrets are all we have left. They keep us grounded, remind us of what we've done, what we can't undo."

Kael shook his head gently, his eyes searching hers. "Or they trap us. They keep us here, holding onto shadows instead of facing what's real." He turned another page of the tome, reading aloud, "I loved him too late, held back my words until they became chains. I thought I was protecting myself... but all I did was build my own prison."

Lira looked down, her voice barely a whisper. "I know that feeling."

Kael reached out, covering her hand with his. "Then tell me, Lira. Tell me what you're holding onto."

Her eyes met his, filled with hesitation and the weight of a sorrow she'd kept buried for so long. "There was someone... his name was Corin. He was... everything. Brave, loyal... he trusted me with his life." She took a deep breath, her voice trembling. "And I failed him. He trusted me to keep him safe, and I couldn't. I lost him, Kael. I watched him slip away, and I couldn't... I couldn't do anything to save him."

Kael's expression softened, empathy clear in his gaze. "Lira... losing someone you care about, it's... it changes you. But carrying that guilt alone, shutting everyone out because of it... that's exactly what Varunel wants. It's what keeps us trapped."

She swallowed, struggling to keep her voice steady. "You don't understand. Corin believed in me, believed that I could keep him safe. And after he was gone, all I had left was that guilt. It became this... shield. I thought if I carried it, maybe I wouldn't fail anyone else."

Kael moved closer, his hand still resting on hers. "But that guilt isn't protecting you, Lira. It's keeping you from living, from letting anyone in. It's keeping you in the past, locked in a moment you can't change. You've been carrying this for so long, and it's time to let it go."

She looked away, her voice tinged with bitterness. "And if I let it go? What then? Do I just pretend like it didn't happen, like I didn't fail him? Like I didn't love him?"

Kael shook his head, his voice gentle. "Letting go doesn't mean forgetting him. It doesn't mean pretending he didn't matter. It means honoring his memory by allowing yourself to live, to love, to trust again. By not letting his memory become a chain that keeps you locked in the past."

Her eyes filled with unshed tears, the weight of his words sinking in. "I don't know if I can. I've kept this part of myself hidden for so long. It's... it's safer that way."

"But are you happy?" he asked, his voice a quiet challenge. "Are you really living, or just surviving? Lira, I don't want to lose you to this place, to a curse built on regrets and broken promises. I want us to face this together, to walk out of here free."

She took a shaky breath, her hand tightening around his. "Corin... he was my light, Kael. He showed me what it was to believe in something, to trust in someone else. And when he was gone, it felt like I'd lost that part of myself."

Kael's thumb brushed over her knuckles, grounding her. "Maybe he was your light once. But that doesn't mean you have to stay in darkness now. You have a choice, Lira. You can carry his memory forward without letting it consume you. You can let yourself feel... without being afraid."

She looked at him, her voice raw, vulnerable. "And what if I'm too afraid? What if I can't let go?"

"Then I'll be here," he said simply. "As long as it takes. I'll be here, beside you, reminding you that you're not alone. You don't have to carry his memory by yourself. I'm here to help you honor it... to help you move forward."

For the first time, she let herself lean into his touch, her walls crumbling just enough to let the weight of her grief slip free. "Thank you, Kael," she whispered, her voice filled with a quiet, trembling hope. "Thank you for not giving up on me."

His fingers tightened around hers, a gentle promise. "I'm not giving up on us, Lira. Not now. Not ever."

And as they sat together, the shadows around them seemed to draw back, retreating in the face of the quiet strength they'd found in each other. The tome lay open between them, the voices of Varunel's lost souls fading into silence, as if, for the first time, they'd found a peace within the darkness.

Lira sat close beside Kael, her usual guarded expression softened, the weight of her confession still settling between them. For the first time, she didn't feel the need to pull away, to retreat into the walls she had spent years building. Instead, she felt a strange lightness, as if sharing her grief had loosened the chains Varunel had so carefully woven around her.

Kael's gaze remained steady, a quiet warmth in his eyes as he watched her. His voice was soft, patient. "Lira, you don't have to hide anymore. Not from me."

She hesitated, her gaze dropping, as though she were struggling to find the words. "It's strange. I've spent so long keeping everything inside, thinking it was… safer that way. That no one could hurt me if they didn't know the real me. But now, sitting here, it feels like… like maybe it was hurting me more."

He nodded, understanding etched into his expression. "Sometimes, letting someone in feels like the most dangerous thing we can do. But it's also… it's freeing. You don't have to carry everything alone."

Her eyes met his, and in that moment, the last of her defenses fell away. "You're right. I think... I think I've always known that. But admitting it—trusting it—that's different. I've pushed people away because I thought I had to be strong. For Corin, for myself... for everyone who depended on me. And now, here you are, refusing to leave no matter how many walls I throw up."

Kael smiled, his voice filled with gentle amusement. "I'm stubborn like that. You'll have to get used to it."

A laugh escaped her, surprising them both. It was soft, almost shy, as though she were rediscovering a part of herself that had been buried beneath years of pain. "Well, I'm starting to realize that maybe I like stubborn."

His fingers brushed hers, tentative but warm. "Then you're in trouble. Because I'm not going anywhere, Lira. Not now, not ever."

She looked down, her cheeks flushed, the vulnerability in her eyes unmistakable. "I never thought I'd say this, Kael, but... I'm glad you didn't give up on me. I didn't think anyone would be willing to break through these walls. I didn't think anyone would care enough to try."

Kael's gaze softened, his hand gently covering hers. "I care, Lira. And I don't need you to be perfect, or fearless, or invulnerable. I just need you to be real with me. To let me stand beside you, even if it means facing every shadow this city throws at us."

Her fingers curled around his, the connection between them a quiet promise, fragile but undeniable. "Then I'll try. I don't know how, but I'll try. For you… and maybe even for me."

He leaned in slightly, his voice a whisper. "That's all I could ever ask for."

They sat in silence, the weight of their words lingering in the air, a newfound closeness binding them. And for the first time since entering Varunel, the city's oppressive presence seemed to wane, as if their connection was a force strong enough to push back the darkness, to weaken the hold of the shadows.

Lira looked up, her eyes searching his face, a small, tentative smile breaking through. "Maybe this city… maybe it can't win against something like this. Something real."

Kael's smile mirrored hers, filled with a hope that felt like sunlight breaking through the fog. "Then we won't let it. We'll hold on to this… to each other. And Varunel can keep its shadows. We have something stronger."

Their hands remained entwined, a quiet moment of trust, of connection that was stronger than any curse, any fear. For the first time, Lira felt that maybe, just maybe, there was a way out of Varunel—a path not marked by darkness or regret, but by something fragile, something beautiful, something real.

The chamber grew quiet, the oppressive weight of Varunel lifting, if only slightly. The shadows that had lurked so heavily, pressing against their every step, seemed to pull back, granting them a brief, tentative peace. The mist that had hung thick in the air softened, and for the first time, a faint warmth seemed to filter through the silence.

Lira took a deep breath, feeling the strange, rare lightness in her chest. She looked over at Kael, his face relaxed, an unguarded expression in his eyes that mirrored her own. For a moment, it was as if the city itself had acknowledged their small victory, offering a fleeting truce.

"Feels different, doesn't it?" she said softly, almost hesitant to break the silence. "Like… like it's giving us space to breathe."

Kael nodded, his gaze sweeping over the chamber. "Maybe Varunel respects what happened here. Maybe… it's allowing us this peace, just for a moment."

She smiled faintly, the corners of her mouth lifting in a way that felt unfamiliar, almost foreign. "It's strange, isn't it? To feel like the city isn't breathing down our necks for once."

He chuckled, the sound low and warm. "Strange, yes. But I'll take it. Even if it's just for a moment." His gaze softened as he looked at her, his voice dipping to a gentler tone. "You look… lighter, Lira. Like a weight's been lifted."

She glanced away, a hint of color rising to her cheeks. "I suppose it has. I'm not… used to feeling like this. Like maybe there's a way through all of this that doesn't involve endless fighting."

Kael's expression grew thoughtful. "Maybe that's exactly what Varunel wants us to see. To realize that sometimes, the only way out is through—through the past, through the pain, through whatever's been holding us back."

Lira's gaze drifted to the open tome between them, the pages still filled with the stories of those who had come before them, who had let their own doubts and regrets keep them bound within Varunel's walls. "If that's true," she murmured, "then facing what we've both buried… it's the only way to break this curse, isn't it?"

Kael nodded, his hand brushing hers, grounding her. "I think so. We've both been haunted by things we couldn't let go of. But… now, maybe we're finally strong enough to face them."

A silence settled between them, a peaceful, shared understanding. Lira felt the warmth of his hand on hers, a steady presence that reminded her she didn't have to walk this path alone. For so long, she had believed strength meant carrying everything herself, that letting someone in was a weakness. But here, with Kael beside her, she felt the quiet strength that came from trusting, from letting someone share the weight she had held for so long.

After a moment, she looked at him, her voice soft but resolute. "Whatever Varunel asks of us… whatever it takes to break free from this place, I'm ready to face it. With you."

Kael's hand tightened around hers, a gentle promise in his gaze. "Then we'll face it together. Whatever darkness is left, whatever the city demands… we'll confront it. And we'll find our way out."

They sat there in the silence, the weight of the city momentarily lifted, their hands intertwined, a quiet resolve settling over them. It was a fragile peace, a calm before the final storm Varunel had in store. But for now, they had this reprieve, this moment of connection that was stronger than any curse or shadow.

And for the first time, they felt the faint, fragile hope that perhaps, just perhaps, Varunel's grip could be broken.

Chapter 14
The Threshold of Despair

The boundary loomed before them, a shimmering veil that stretched as far as the eye could see, marking the edge of Varunel's hold. The early dawn light filtered through the mist, casting an otherworldly glow over the barrier, as if the city itself were watching, waiting to see what they would do. In Lira's hand, the Forgotten Key felt warm, almost alive, its faint glow mirroring the barrier's light.

Kael looked at the boundary, his chest tightening as realization settled over him. This was it—their final chance, their last moment to make things right and leave Varunel's darkness behind. But as he glanced at Lira, a thought struck him, sharp and painful, tugging at something deep within.

"Lira..." he began, his voice filled with an unspoken weight. "Do you feel it? This... this place, it's not going to let us both go, not without a price."

She turned to him, her eyes searching his face, a mixture of determination and fear in her gaze. "What are you saying, Kael? We have the key. We're here. We just... we just need to use it and get out of here."

He swallowed, forcing himself to meet her gaze. "You heard the whispers, the warnings. Varunel thrives on sacrifice, on the unbroken vows and regrets of those it's claimed. It's not going to just let go of both of us without... without taking something in return."

She shook her head, her grip tightening around the key. "No. We've come too far for that. We're not leaving anyone behind, Kael. We do this together."

Kael's hand rested on her shoulder, a gentle but firm touch. "Lira, if there's a way to get you out, to break this curse... I need you to take it. Don't think about what it means for me. This was always about freeing you, about giving you a chance to let go of everything that's haunted you."

Her eyes widened, a flash of anger and desperation crossing her face. "No. Don't you dare do this, Kael. I didn't let you in, didn't fight all these shadows just to lose you now. This isn't some... some noble sacrifice. This is our freedom. Together."

He smiled, though there was sadness in his eyes. "Lira, you've given me something I never thought I'd find in a place like this. You made me believe in something real. And if that means giving up my own freedom so you can have yours... then that's a choice I'm willing to make."

She stepped closer, her voice fierce, her eyes glistening. "I didn't ask you to make that choice, Kael. You can't just decide to leave me behind, like... like it's some sort of gift. You're not a sacrifice. You're my... you're my friend. And I won't walk through that barrier if it means losing you."

His expression softened, a faint hint of a smile breaking through his sorrow. "Lira, I want you to live. I want you to be free of this place, to carry forward everything we fought for. I don't want you to be another story bound to Varunel. This city has taken too much from you already."

She looked down, her fingers brushing over the key, her shoulders trembling. "Then we do this together. Whatever Varunel demands, we face it together. I'm not giving up on you, Kael. Not now. Not ever."

Kael reached out, his hand resting over hers on the key, his voice steady. "Then let's find a way. If this city wants to demand something from us, we'll face it on our own terms. But, Lira… promise me that if it comes down to it, you won't let this place trap you again."

Her gaze was fierce, unwavering. "I'm not leaving without you. That's my promise."

A silence settled between them, the weight of their words hanging in the mist-filled air, as if even Varunel were pausing, waiting. The boundary shimmered, pulsing faintly, and they could feel the city's presence intensify, an almost palpable force pressing against their hearts, testing their resolve.

Kael took a deep breath, his fingers intertwined with hers around the key. "Whatever happens, we'll face it together. And we'll make sure Varunel's hold ends here, once and for all."

She nodded, her expression filled with a fierce determination. "Together. No matter what this place demands."

They stepped forward, their hands entwined, their hearts resolute. And as the boundary pulsed, as if acknowledging the strength of their bond, Varunel's shadows recoiled slightly, sensing, perhaps, that this was a union it could not easily sever.

They stood at the edge of Varunel's boundary, the shimmering barrier casting a ghostly light over them. Kael's gaze lingered on Lira, his expression unreadable, a strange calm settling over him. Lira gripped the Forgotten Key tightly, her pulse racing as she studied the barrier that separated them from freedom—and everything Varunel held them back from. A part of her felt the victory within reach, but the other sensed the city's dark intentions, a price hovering just out of sight.

Kael took a slow breath, his voice breaking the silence. "Lira, there's something I need to say before we… before we take this final step."

She turned to him, catching the seriousness in his gaze, a look that made her heart clench. "What is it?"

He took her hand in his, his thumb brushing over her knuckles as though he were memorizing the feel of her touch. "I don't want you to think I'm giving up, but… if there's a choice here, if Varunel is demanding one of us to stay behind, I want it to be me."

She stared at him, disbelief and frustration mingling in her expression. "What are you saying? Kael, we're almost there. We're finally here, together. Don't… don't even consider staying behind."

He managed a small smile, a bittersweet curve of his lips. "This isn't about giving up. It's about making sure you get the freedom you deserve. I'd rather know you're out there, living, than watch this city claim you. Lira… you've already given enough."

The weight of his words settled over her, pulling at emotions she'd kept locked away, fear twisting with the realization of what he was offering. "Kael, no. You can't just… you can't just decide that. You can't make this choice for me."

He held her gaze, unwavering, his voice gentle but resolute. "Lira, I made this choice the moment I decided to stand beside you. You taught me how to face my own shadows, how to keep fighting even when everything felt lost. And if my staying behind means you get to walk away free… then that's a price I'm willing to pay."

She shook her head, her voice trembling as her defenses crumbled. "Kael, don't. I don't want that. I don't want to leave here without you. You think I came this far just to watch you sacrifice yourself?"

His hand moved to her face, a tender touch that made her heart ache. "It's not a sacrifice, Lira. It's my choice. And it's one I'd make over and over again, for you."

She closed her eyes, fighting back the tears that threatened to spill. "But… but I need you. I don't want to face the world without you. I don't know if I can."

"Lira," he whispered, his voice a mix of strength and sorrow, "you're stronger than you think. And you've already taught me more than you know. You'll be okay. And you'll carry this with you, this... connection, even if we're not both standing on the other side."

Her hand tightened around his, the weight of his words breaking through her last defenses. "Don't ask me to leave you, Kael. I... I care about you. More than I thought I was capable of. Don't make me walk away from that."

His thumb brushed a stray tear from her cheek, his gaze filled with a warmth that left her breathless. "Then don't think of it as leaving. Think of it as carrying a part of me with you. And know that I'll always be here, in some way, no matter what."

The shimmering boundary seemed to pulse in response, as though Varunel itself was absorbing his selfless offer, tightening its grip, urging one of them to surrender. But as Lira looked at him, her heart racing, her voice broke through her fear.

"Kael... please, don't let this city take you from me. We've come too far, and I don't want to go back to a life without you. Not now, not ever."

He took a shaky breath, his own resolve faltering as he looked at her, the depth of her feelings, the vulnerability in her eyes breaking through his resolve. "Lira, I... I didn't expect to feel this way either. But if there's any chance of you leaving, of you breaking free, I want to give that to you."

She shook her head, her voice raw with emotion. "We'll find another way. Together. We'll face whatever Varunel throws at us, but I'm not losing you. Not now."

A silence settled between them, filled with the weight of unspoken promises, of fears laid bare. And as they stood, side by side, the city seemed to hold its breath, its dark intentions momentarily held back by the strength of their connection.

The boundary shimmered before them, casting a pale, unearthly light across their faces. The weight of Kael's offer hung in the air, thick and unyielding, like Varunel itself was testing their resolve. Lira's heart pounded, her chest tight as she grappled with the impossible choice he had laid before her. She looked at him, his gaze steady, unwavering, but behind it, she saw the quiet pain, the silent goodbye he was preparing himself to make.

"No," she whispered, her voice cracking. She reached for his hand, clasping it tightly, like it was the only thing grounding her in this moment. "No, Kael. You don't get to make this choice for me. I won't let you stay behind."

"Lira…" His voice was gentle, the calm resolve in his eyes like a knife to her heart. "It's my choice. I'm doing this because I want you to be free. You've given me more than I ever thought I'd find in this place—hope, strength. I can live with this if it means you get to walk away whole."

Tears threatened to spill as she tightened her grip on his hand, her voice trembling. "You don't understand. You're part of me now, Kael. I can't walk through that barrier and pretend any of this didn't happen. I don't want to be free if it means losing you."

He swallowed, his expression softening. "Lira, I need you to live. I need you to be free of all this weight. You've been carrying it for so long… you deserve a life beyond these shadows."

She shook her head, stepping closer, the vulnerability she'd hidden for so long cracking open. "I don't want that life without you. I don't want any of this freedom if it means losing the one person who's ever seen me, really seen me. Don't ask me to leave you here. I… I love you, Kael. Do you understand? I love you."

His breath caught, surprise flickering in his eyes, quickly replaced by a fierce determination. "Lira… I—"

"No," she cut him off, her voice growing stronger, fueled by the emotions she'd kept hidden for so long. "I need you to understand. I was ready to fight my way out of here, to keep going alone, to push through whatever Varunel threw at us. But that was before you. You changed everything, Kael. You made me believe again, made me want something beyond this cursed place."

He looked at her, his eyes filled with a mixture of wonder and disbelief. "Lira, I didn't know… I didn't think you—"

"Because I was terrified," she admitted, her voice breaking. "I was terrified of feeling this way, of letting someone in. I thought it would make me weak, that caring about someone would only end in pain. But you've shown me... you've shown me that strength doesn't mean standing alone. It means being willing to fight for the people we love."

Kael's hand trembled slightly in hers, his voice thick. "Lira... you don't know how much I wanted to hear you say that. But if it comes at the cost of your freedom... if loving me means you're trapped here, I can't live with that. I won't let you be another soul bound to Varunel."

She shook her head, her gaze fierce, unwavering. "If that's what Varunel demands, then I'm willing to pay it. I'm willing to stay, Kael, if it means being with you. Because losing you... that would be worse than any curse."

He stared at her, his resolve crumbling under the weight of her words. "Lira... you don't have to stay. I don't want you to stay because you're afraid of losing me. I want you to live."

"I am living," she whispered, her hand lifting to his cheek, her thumb tracing the line of his jaw. "For the first time, I feel alive, Kael. I'm tired of running, of hiding, of pretending I don't care. I'm here, and I'm with you. That's all I need."

A silence fell between them, heavy with emotion, the city's power seeming to falter, its shadows recoiling as if in the face of their honesty. Kael leaned into her touch, his voice barely above a whisper. "Lira, I never thought… I never imagined you'd feel this way."

Her lips curved in a sad smile, her hand still resting against his cheek. "Neither did I. But here we are, on the edge of everything, and I've never been more certain of anything in my life."

He closed his eyes, his hand covering hers, his voice thick with emotion. "Then we'll face this together. Whatever Varunel asks of us, whatever it demands… we'll stand against it. And we'll find a way out. Together."

The boundary shimmered before them, its light wavering as though challenged by their words, by the love they had finally dared to confess. For the first time, Varunel felt less like a prison and more like a test—a test of their strength, their honesty, their willingness to confront the deepest parts of themselves.

Lira took a deep breath, her fingers laced tightly with his, her gaze steady. "Then let's do this. Let's face whatever comes. No more running, no more hiding. Just… us."

Kael nodded, his voice a quiet promise. "Just us."

And as they turned to face the boundary, united in their resolve, Varunel seemed to shudder, its shadows retreating as though it, too, felt the power of their connection, the strength of two souls bound by love and unafraid of whatever lay ahead.

A tremor pulsed through Varunel, shaking the ground beneath them, as though the city itself was resisting the strength of their bond. Lira and Kael stood hand in hand, their unspoken vows, their promises to each other filling the air, pressing against the darkness that had loomed over Varunel for so long. The boundary shimmered before them, its once-unbreakable surface now rippling as if unsure, hesitant.

Kael's voice was low, his words steady but brimming with emotion. "Lira… whatever happens, I want you to know, you've given me something I never thought I'd find in this place. You've shown me what it is to love, to feel something more than fear or survival."

Lira squeezed his hand, her gaze fierce and unyielding. "You were never just someone to survive with, Kael. You're the one who broke down my walls, the one who showed me that there's more to life than just fighting ghosts. I won't lose you now, not to Varunel, not to anything."

As if in response to her words, the boundary shuddered, the once-solid shadows around them seeming to fray at the edges, dissolving into wisps of mist that retreated into the walls. A faint light began to pierce through, small but unmistakable, cutting through the darkness that had surrounded them for so long.

Kael's eyes widened, his gaze flickering to the light that now illuminated the gate. "Do you see that? It's… it's as if the city is letting us go."

Lira let out a breath, a mix of disbelief and hope crossing her face. "Maybe it's more than that. Maybe Varunel was bound by those who couldn't let go of their own pain, their own regrets. But we… we chose to face it together."

He turned to her, his voice filled with wonder. "Our love broke the curse, Lira. We did this. We fought through Varunel's shadows, and now it's… it's finally releasing us."

The light continued to spread, chasing away the remaining shadows, revealing the gates that had once barred them from freedom. Slowly, the gates creaked open, a path appearing beyond, leading out of Varunel's twisted labyrinth. They could feel the city loosening its grip, as if the very fabric of its curse was unraveling, undone by the strength of their connection.

Lira's voice was a soft murmur, filled with awe. "It's giving us a way out. After everything… after all we've endured, Varunel is finally letting us go."

Kael pulled her close, his hand still entwined with hers. "Then let's take it. Let's walk out of here together, free."

But as they took their first steps toward the gate, Varunel's shadows seemed to gather one last time, coalescing into a single form, a faint, ghostly presence that hovered before them. It was the essence of the city itself, an echo of the souls it had trapped, the love it had twisted.

A whisper filled the air, faint but clear, a final plea. "You have broken the cycle… but remember, love is a promise, one that can heal or bind. Honor it, or face the fate of those who failed before you."

Kael met the shadow's gaze, a flicker of sorrow in his eyes as he nodded. "We understand. Love isn't something we'll take for granted. We'll honor it… as those before us couldn't."

The shadow seemed to sigh, its form unraveling, dissipating into the air. As it vanished, the light grew brighter, filling every corner of Varunel, washing away the darkness that had claimed so many. The curse that had held the city in its thrall for centuries was finally lifting, the weight of forgotten promises and broken hearts dissolving into the dawn.

Lira turned to Kael, her voice choked with emotion. "We're free, Kael. We're really free."

He smiled, pulling her close, his forehead resting against hers. "Yes, we are. And we'll carry this with us, the love that set us free."

Hand in hand, they stepped forward, passing through the gates as the light enveloped them, casting Varunel in a warmth it hadn't known in ages. And as they crossed the threshold, they felt the weight of their pasts fall away, leaving only the hope of a future, together, beyond the city's walls.

Chapter 15
The Last Whisper

The first slivers of dawn crept over the horizon, casting a warm, golden glow over Varunel's darkened ruins. As Lira and Kael stepped out of the city's gates, a wave of light broke across the land, sweeping away the shadows that had haunted them for so long. For a moment, they both stood in silence, taking in the sight of Varunel behind them, its walls no longer looming with the threat of eternal entrapment but softened, fading into the background as the curse finally lifted.

Kael released a breath he hadn't realized he was holding, turning to Lira, his voice filled with wonder. "We... we actually did it. We're out. It's over."

Lira's gaze remained fixed on the city, her expression a mixture of relief and disbelief. "It doesn't even feel real, does it? After everything... it's like I'm waiting for Varunel to pull us back, to tell us it was just another trick."

He shook his head, a faint smile breaking through his exhaustion. "If that were true, I think we'd know by now. The curse... it's really gone. We broke it, Lira. You broke it."

She looked down, her voice barely a whisper. "Not just me. I couldn't have done it without you, Kael. If you hadn't been there, if you hadn't..." She hesitated, searching his face, as though still trying to grasp the reality of their escape. "If you hadn't believed in us, I think I'd still be trapped back there, tangled in my own shadows."

He reached out, his hand finding hers, a warmth that felt even brighter than the dawn breaking around them. "I believed in you because you gave me a reason to. You showed me there's more than just surviving… there's actually living. And with you… that feels possible."

A smile tugged at her lips, tentative but real. "I spent so long running from things, hiding in walls of my own making. But here… with you, I felt like I could finally let those walls fall."

He laughed softly, his voice thick with relief. "And here I thought I was the one following your lead. You've shown me more strength than I thought possible. You didn't just face Varunel… you faced everything you kept hidden."

Her gaze softened, her fingers tightening around his. "Because of you, Kael. I think I would've stayed hidden forever if you hadn't challenged me. If you hadn't refused to let me carry that weight alone."

They both looked back at the city one last time, the walls that had once held such menace now seeming to blend into the landscape, losing their power, returning to mere stone and shadow as the first full light of day crept over them.

Kael let out a long breath, his hand still linked with hers. "I don't know what lies ahead. But I know I don't want to face it alone. Not anymore."

Lira's eyes met his, her voice filled with a quiet certainty. "Neither do I. I think… I think I've finally found something worth staying for. Someone worth fighting for."

They shared a look, a mutual understanding passing between them, as if Varunel's shadows had cemented something that even the dawn couldn't wash away. They had faced their fears, their pasts, and had come out on the other side, bound not by curse but by choice.

"Then let's go," Kael murmured, pulling her close, his voice a promise and a plea. "Let's see what the world looks like… together."

Hand in hand, they turned from Varunel's gates, walking into the dawn, their footsteps lighter, the weight of the curse finally lifted from their shoulders. And as the city faded into the distance, only the warmth of morning remained, carrying them forward into the new day.

The village of Hollowbrook seemed quieter than they remembered, softened in the pale light of morning. As Lira and Kael made their way through the familiar streets, they felt the subtle shift in themselves, like they'd left pieces of who they once were back in Varunel. The weight of that cursed city, the darkness that had pressed on them, was now a memory—one they carried together.

Waiting at the edge of the village, Elder Thorne stood beneath the old willow tree, her silver hair catching the first rays of dawn. She watched their approach with a serene expression, her eyes reflecting a quiet, knowing wisdom. There was a faint smile on her lips, one that seemed to see straight through them, as if she knew exactly what they'd endured to return here.

Kael gave a nod of greeting, his voice carrying a mixture of relief and reverence. "Elder Thorne… we did it. We made it out."

The elder tilted her head, her smile widening just a bit. "So I see. I felt it when the curse lifted, like a shadow passing away from Hollowbrook itself. You've brought peace to Varunel… and to yourselves, I think."

Lira shifted beside him, her fingers brushing against Kael's before she reached for his hand with a quiet, intentional strength. "It wasn't easy. Varunel doesn't let go without a fight."

Elder Thorne nodded, her gaze softening as she looked at their joined hands. "Breaking such a curse requires more than just courage. It requires a willingness to confront what lies beneath—the things we hold closest and hide deepest." Her eyes sparkled with understanding. "It seems you both found something worth holding on to."

Kael glanced at Lira, a warmth flooding his chest as he met her gaze. "I found someone who showed me how to let go of my own shadows… and how to make room for something better."

Lira's lips curved in a soft smile, her voice low but filled with conviction. "And I found someone who made me realize that strength isn't in solitude… but in letting someone in, even when it's terrifying."

The elder's smile deepened, her expression one of quiet pride. "Love has a way of illuminating even the darkest paths. The bond between you both... it's stronger than any curse. Varunel's magic could not withstand it."

Kael squeezed Lira's hand, his voice filled with quiet wonder. "I didn't think... I didn't think I'd find this kind of strength in another person. Lira showed me something I'd been too afraid to look for on my own. She changed me."

Lira looked at him, a flicker of vulnerability in her eyes. "And you... you reminded me that life isn't something to survive alone. You've become a part of me, Kael. And I don't intend to let that go."

Elder Thorne reached out, placing a gentle hand over their joined ones. "Hold on to each other, then. Varunel tested you both, and you've come through it stronger. What you carry now... it's rare, precious. Don't take it lightly."

Kael nodded, his hand tightening around Lira's, as if to seal the promise between them. "We won't. I think... we're finally ready to leave the past behind."

Lira looked down, her voice soft. "It's strange. I thought letting go would feel like losing something. But now, it feels like I've finally found myself."

Elder Thorne's smile was warm, knowing. "Because you have. The pieces of you that were hidden away, held back—they're free now. Varunel has no more hold on you."

Kael looked toward the sunrise, a new light in his eyes. "Thank you, Elder. For helping us see what we needed to find, even if it was buried in shadows."

The elder inclined her head, her gaze gentle. "The path was yours to walk. I only pointed the way. And now, you must decide where it leads."

They exchanged a look, a silent understanding passing between them, an unspoken promise for the future. And as they turned away from Hollowbrook, with the elder's blessing behind them, they felt the full weight of their freedom—a life beyond shadows, beyond Varunel's curse, a life they would face together.

The morning sun spread its warmth across Hollowbrook, casting gentle light on the village's quiet streets as if the dawn itself were bidding them farewell. Lira and Kael walked side by side, a comfortable silence settling between them as they passed by the familiar sights, the echoes of their first steps here fading into memory. For the first time in what felt like an eternity, they walked without the shadows pressing in, without the weight of Varunel's curse on their shoulders.

They paused at the edge of town, where the path forked, one road leading back to the world they'd left and the other winding into the unknown. The air felt lighter here, like a promise of something untouched by the darkness they'd just escaped.

Kael shifted, glancing over at Lira with a soft smile. "So, what now? Our mission… it was never really about Varunel, was it? At least, not in the way we thought."

Lira took a breath, her gaze fixed on the horizon, the possibilities stretching out before her in a way they never had before. "No, I suppose not. It feels strange, doesn't it? To have come through all that, only to find… freedom, but without any clear direction."

He nodded, his expression thoughtful. "Maybe that's the point. We have a chance to choose now, to make something of our own. No mission, no curse, just… whatever we decide to be."

She looked at him, a faint, tentative smile breaking through the guarded expression she wore so well. "And what do you think that should be, Kael? What does the future look like to you?"

Kael held her gaze, the intensity of his sincerity shining through. "Together. Whatever we decide, I want to face it with you, Lira. I know we came to Hollowbrook as strangers, and maybe we leave a little more than that. But I'd like to see where this goes. Us."

Her heart skipped, the weight of his words settling over her with a warmth that chased away the last of her fears. "Together," she repeated softly, almost to herself. She looked away, back toward the path, her voice quieter. "I think… I think I'd like that too."

A silence fell, one filled with an unspoken understanding, a promise woven between them that needed no words. They'd faced their own darkness, wrestled with the weight of their pasts, and come through the other side with something more than they had bargained for. Something worth holding onto.

"Then let's go," Kael said, his voice steady, carrying a hint of wonder. He reached out, his hand brushing against hers, a small but deliberate touch that felt like the first step into this unknown future.

Lira met his gaze, her own resolve breaking into a full smile, one that held the faintest edge of vulnerability. She reached out, her fingers intertwining with his, her voice clear and soft. "Let's go."

And with that, they turned toward the road that led away from Hollowbrook, away from Varunel and everything it had once represented. They walked forward, together, their footsteps in perfect rhythm, an unspoken bond carrying them into the dawn of a new life, with the promise of a future they would forge side by side.

The path from Hollowbrook stretched out before them, bathed in the soft glow of the dawn that broke steadily over the horizon. It was the first true sunrise over Varunel in centuries, a light that cast warmth and peace over the land, dissolving the city's lingering shadows. The golden hues of morning spread across the sky, painting the clouds in shades of rose and amber, a sight so beautiful and rare it felt like a gift, a blessing after all they'd endured.

Lira walked beside Kael, her gaze flicking up to the sky before settling on him, her voice thoughtful. "I never thought I'd see this place... at peace. I didn't even think it was possible."

Kael looked at her, his expression filled with quiet wonder. "Neither did I. But maybe that's what we gave Varunel—the chance to rest, finally. It feels different, doesn't it? Like the city itself has found closure."

She nodded, her eyes distant as she looked back toward where the city lay hidden beyond the hills, the weight of its curse finally lifted. "For so long, I thought that strength meant standing alone, pushing through no matter what. But Varunel taught me that sometimes, it's about letting someone stand with you, even in the shadows." She paused, glancing at him. "You showed me that."

He reached over, his fingers finding hers, giving her hand a gentle squeeze. "And you taught me that love doesn't make us weaker. It's not something to fear or avoid. It's... a strength all its own. One that can break even the strongest curses."

A faint smile touched her lips, her fingers tightening around his. "So where do we go from here, Kael? The mission we started with... it feels so small now, like it was never what mattered."

He chuckled softly, his eyes warm as they traced her face. "Then let's make a new mission. One where we decide the path. One where we don't have to follow orders or face curses. Just... us, seeing where this road leads."

She laughed, a sound so rare from her own lips that it surprised them both. "You make it sound so simple."

"Maybe it is," he said, smiling. "For the first time, there's no curse, no city with dark secrets, no walls to keep us apart. Just you and me."

She looked at him, her voice quiet, vulnerable. "You know, I don't think I ever allowed myself to want something like this. I always thought letting someone in would just… lead to more loss. But with you, Kael… I think I'm ready. Ready to see what's out there."

His eyes softened, a hint of emotion breaking through his usual steady expression. "Then let's make that our new dawn, Lira. Let's write our own story, not one bound by shadows or regret, but one where we get to live."

They continued down the path, the village of Hollowbrook disappearing behind them, and with each step, they felt the weight of Varunel fade, replaced by a growing lightness that settled over them. The bond they'd forged in the darkness now felt like something sacred, a quiet strength they carried within them, each other's presence like a steadying anchor.

Lira glanced over her shoulder one last time, the city a faint silhouette in the distance. She felt no sorrow, no fear—just a sense of peace. "Goodbye, Varunel," she murmured, her voice filled with a calm resolve. "Thank you… for everything you taught us."

Kael smiled, understanding her sentiment. "Here's to a life beyond shadows, beyond fear." He looked at her, his gaze steady and filled with warmth. "And here's to us."

She nodded, her smile widening, her hand still clasped in his as they stepped into the dawn together. "To us."

And as the first full light of morning spilled across the landscape, they left behind the ruins, the darkness, and the unspoken sorrow of Varunel, walking toward a future they would build hand in hand, forever changed by the city—and by the love they had discovered in its shadows.

Epilogue
Beyond the Mist

The air beyond the Veiled Gates was lighter, fresher, carrying the faint scent of wildflowers and damp earth. Lira and Kael emerged into the early dawn, their clothes tattered, their faces pale, but their steps steady. The mist of Varunel lingered behind them, reluctant to release its hold, as if the city itself mourned their departure.

Kael stumbled slightly on the uneven path, his hand brushing against Lira's arm for balance. "We made it," he said, his voice hoarse, barely more than a whisper.

"Barely," Lira replied, her tone measured, though the weariness in her eyes betrayed her. She scanned the horizon, her hand instinctively resting on the talisman around her neck. The weight of the city's memories was still heavy on her shoulders.

Kael stopped, turning back toward the gates. The towering arches loomed in the distance, veiled in their ever-present mist. Even from here, he could feel the city's presence, a shadow that would follow them long after they left. "Do you think it'll let us go?" he asked, his voice tinged with uncertainty.

Lira didn't answer immediately. Her fingers tightened around the talisman, its carvings cool against her skin. "It doesn't matter," she said finally. "We're out. That's all that counts."

Kael frowned, his gaze lingering on the gates. "I'm not sure it's that simple."

"It never is," Lira admitted, starting down the path. "But we can't let it pull us back."

He hesitated, then followed, his steps slower, heavier. The weight of Varunel's secrets clung to him, the voices and shadows lingering at the edge of his mind. "You think anyone will believe us?" he asked after a long silence.

"About what?" Lira asked, her tone flat.

"About the city. The whispers. The…" He trailed off, struggling to find the words. "Everything."

"They won't have to," Lira said simply. "We know what happened. That's enough."

Kael sighed, glancing at her. "For you, maybe. But I can't just pretend none of it mattered."

She stopped, turning to face him. Her expression was unreadable, her dark eyes steady. "It mattered," she said quietly. "More than either of us can understand right now. But dwelling on it won't help."

Kael studied her for a moment, then nodded reluctantly. "You're right," he said softly. "But it still feels like we left something behind."

Lira's gaze flicked toward the horizon, where the first rays of sunlight pierced through the mist. "We did," she said. "But we brought something out with us, too."

He followed her gaze, his eyes narrowing. "What do you mean?"

She didn't answer immediately. Instead, she pulled the talisman from around her neck, holding it out to him. The carvings shimmered faintly in the light, their patterns shifting like ripples on water. "The city gave us this for a reason," she said. "We just have to figure out why."

Kael hesitated, then took the talisman, its weight grounding him. "You're not going to miss it?"

Lira's lips twitched into a faint smirk. "I've had my share of cursed artifacts for one lifetime."

He chuckled softly, tucking the talisman into his pack. "Fair enough. But what do we do now?"

"We move forward," Lira said simply, starting down the path again. "There's more out there than Varunel. And now we know how to face it."

Kael watched her for a moment, then followed, his steps lighter than before. The whispers of the city faded as they walked, replaced by the gentle rustle of leaves and the chirping of birds. The world beyond Varunel seemed brighter, more vivid, as if reminding them of what they had survived.

As they reached the edge of the forest, Kael glanced back one last time. The Veiled Gates were barely visible now, swallowed by the mist. "Do you think it'll ever let anyone else out?" he asked.

Lira didn't look back. "Maybe," she said. "If they're strong enough."

He nodded, turning to face the open road ahead. The weight of Varunel lingered, but it was no longer suffocating. For the first time in what felt like an eternity, he felt the pull of something else—possibility, hope.

And as they walked away from the cursed city, the sun rising higher with each step, the shadows of Varunel began to fade, leaving only their memories behind.

Milton Keynes UK
Ingram Content Group UK Ltd.
UKHW031342011224
451755UK00001B/205